Pippa Roscoe lives in Norfolk near her family and makes daily promises to herself that *this* is the day she'll leave the computer to take a long walk in the countryside. She can't remember a time when she wasn't dreaming about handsome heroes and innocent heroines. Totally her mother's fault, of course—she gave Pippa her first romance to read at the age of seven! She is inconceivably happy that she gets to share those daydreams with you. Follow her on Twitter @PippaRoscoe.

Also by Pippa Roscoe

Conquering His Virgin Queen

Discover more at millsandboon.co.uk.

A RING TO TAKE
HIS REVENGE

PIPPA ROSCOE

This book is produced from independently certified FSC™
to ensure responsible forest management.
For more information visit www.harpercollins.co.uk/green

Printed and bound in Spain
by CPI, Barcelona

MILLS & BOON

First Published in Great Britain 2018
by Mills & Boon, an imprint of HarperCollins*Publishers*
1 London Bridge Street, London, SE1 9GF

© 2018 Pippa Roscoe

ISBN: 978-0-263-93481-6

For my editor Sareeta.
Thank you for whipping this into shape
and helping me to see the way to a better book.
May it be the first of many!

PROLOGUE

London...

ANTONIO ARCURI GESTURED for the petite brunette to slide into the limousine ahead of him. He might be accustomed to ushering women he'd only just met into his chauffeur-driven town car, but not when it was business. Never when it was business.

Yet there had been no other option. His morning meeting had run unacceptably late, and now he could neither cancel this last interview for a new PA nor be late for his meeting with the other two members of the Winners' Circle—the racing syndicate he co-owned.

Antonio had been waiting almost a year to see his closest friends Dimitri and Danyl, his brothers in more ways than blood could ever account for. So he had been forced to multi-task. And Antonio hated nothing more than having his hand forced.

So far, the brunette—Ms Guilham—had yet even to raise an eyebrow at the somewhat unusual relocation of their meeting, which boded well. The way that she struggled with the wayward hemline of her skirt as it rose up over toned, creamy thighs the moment she sat back on the plush leather seat did not. The hemline that when she was standing bordered on the overly conservative was now a sincerely unwanted distraction.

Settling into the seat beside her, Antonio studied Emma Guilham from the corner of his eye. She was petite. Beautiful, he conceded, then filed and discarded the fact. Whether a future PA of his was attractive or not was irrelevant. At least she had finally stopped fidgeting with her skirt.

The limousine pulled away from the dark underground parking area of his London office, emerged into pale wintry sunlight...and into busy central London traffic. He cursed silently and resisted the urge to glance at his watch. He knew what time it was and he was cutting it fine.

'Your driver should take St James's and then Pall Mall. Christmas and Regent Street don't mix well.'

She locked her hazel eyes on his and Antonio felt a sudden start in his chest. Her gaze held no desperate eagerness to please, no fevered excitement, nor the sensual assessment he often felt when women looked at him. He knew he was attractive and took full advantage of the fact—though never with his employees.

But, most importantly, there was no pretence in her eyes. And that was both unusual and—to him—invaluable.

Compared to the three other interviewees he'd met, she was, on paper, the least impressive. At barely twenty-two, Emma Guilham was young. But while the other candidates had varied in age from late twenties to early fifties, she currently seemed the least flappable. He didn't need to look at her CV. His quick mind recalled all the pertinent information and he proceeded with the interview for the position of his new PA.

'You graduated with your International Business

Studies degree from SOAS after attaining four A levels. You can type one hundred and twenty words per minute, you like travelling and reading,' he stated, somewhat disconcerted to see the hazel flecks in her eyes transition into sea-green foam. 'You are hardworking—a fact repeatedly attested to by the CFO of my London office, where you have been working full-time for the past few months, and part-time for the year before that. At the same time finishing your degree—another thing my CFO repeatedly emphasised.'

A quick nod of the head was Emma's only reaction, which drew a frown to his forehead. Usually candidates like to expound on their virtues when he raised the opportunity to do so. He left a second, a breath of space for her to speak, but she remained silent.

'The position is in New York. I deal in high-stakes, highly confidential business acquisition and I expect long hours, absolute focus and complete discretion. Both in business matters and personal. I am not always present in the New York office, but your presence will be required there full-time.'

'Of course.'

He continued to watch for the smallest change in expression. She had yet to display the excitement or even the badly supressed shock and awe that he had so irritatingly witnessed through the previous interviews.

'You don't seem to be engaging with this interview, Ms Guilham.' He had no patience for time-wasters. And he had no need for a 'yes' woman, but still. This was... unique.

'You have yet to ask me a question, Mr Arcuri,' she said, with no trace of accusation or offence in her tone. 'May I speak plainly?' she asked, and he gestured for her to do so with a swift swipe of his hand.

'Mr Arcuri, I have attended three preliminary interviews for this position—one with UK HR, one with North American HR, and one with your previous PA. I am under no illusions as to my limited experience in comparison to more seasoned applicants, and can only conclude that your willingness to squeeze me in to your "commute" is a gracious courtesy. It is one that I appreciate.'

At this, the brunette rapped on the window to talk to the driver.

'Left here, then second right,' she said, before turning her gaze back to him. 'I believe at this point your choice comes down to personality. And as far as you're concerned, as my future boss, I don't have one. You want someone to live and breathe Arcuri Enterprises? That I can do. You want someone to handle an international diary? I can do it with my eyes closed. You want someone to bar the way and dissolve anything that might prevent your valuable time from being spent as you wish? I'm the one you want. Anything else your background checks can uncover or you don't need to know. I want to work for you because you're the best. It's that simple.'

The limousine glided to a stop outside the grand building of the Asquith Club in London just as Antonio was digesting the rather impressive and somewhat surprising speech that had filled the car.

Ms Guilham smiled, not unkindly.

Antonio felt a small smile pull at the edges of his lips in response.

'I have one question, Ms Guilham.'

'Yes?'

'If you were stranded on a desert island and you were allowed one item, what would it be?'

Antonio had heard many different answers to the question over the years. Mozart's music, the complete works of Shakespeare, a piano. But he'd only ever heard *her* answer once before. It was the one he had given himself.

'A satellite phone.'

He nodded, betraying nothing.

'Mr Arcuri, thank you for the opportunity to speak with you. I shall look forward to hearing from HR and hope that you have an enjoyable lunch. I'll see myself back to the office.'

With that Emma Guilham left Antonio sitting in the car, feeling stunned for the first time in some while. And he wasn't the only one, considering the way his driver was currently watching Emma's departure with something like awe.

As Antonio exited the limousine and made his way to the private room at the Asquith where Dimitri Kyriakou and Danyl Nejem Al Arain waited, he forced his mind away from the way Ms Guilham's hips had swayed as she'd walked towards Piccadilly Circus tube station.

With ruthless efficiency he refocused his mind on the Winners' Circle.

The three men had met as students, and their friendship had been forged in the depths of their darkest moments. Through it all they had supported, commiserated and celebrated with each other. And when, after university, Antonio had needed capital to start his business, Dimitri, Danyl and his maternal grandfather had been his first investors. He had, of course, paid them back with interest, and in half the promised time. But he had never forgotten the debt he owed his friends.

Antonio knew in his heart, in his blood, that he wouldn't be here today without them. And they would say the same of him. And now, after a year, all three men—each of whom regularly featured in the newspapers as some of the greatest living business figures—would finally be together in the same room again.

As he made his way towards the table in the private dining area a small blonde was hastily leaving, casting him with a frowning glance as she passed.

'What did I miss?' Antonio asked, taking in the appearance of his friends.

Wrongful imprisonment had taken its toll on Dimitri, yet his powerful Greek features still turned the heads of any nearby female. And Danyl didn't need to rely on his royal status as Sheikh in line to the Terhren throne. Brooding intensity radiated from him—as Antonio's last assistant had remarked.

Only the might of the American legal system had put a halt to their quarterly meetings—the one immovable feature in Antonio's increasingly full diary. But within the year Dimitri's innocence had been realised and proclaimed, and now they were finally back together again.

'A proposition,' Dimitri replied in response to Antonio's question.

'In public? During the day? Gentlemen, you're putting my scandalous reputation to shame,' Antonio asserted.

'A *professional* proposition,' growled Danyl through gritted teeth.

'She—' nodding to the exit made by the blonde woman '—wants to race for the syndicate in the Hanley Cup,' Dimitri clarified.

'We have a jockey,' interjected Danyl.

'She says she can win all three races.'

Antonio was mildly intrigued. 'That's not been done since...'

'Since her father trained the horse and rider twenty years ago,' supplied Dimitri.

Antonio's mind raced through the implications. '*That* was Mason McAulty?'

A rather undignified grunt emerged from Danyl's direction.

Antonio considered the possibilities...the amount of the winning purse, the attention from the global press. News of their racing syndicate had ebbed and flowed over the years, but no one could argue with the level of their success. Founded shortly after their university days, it had been the perfect venture for three men who loved the high-stakes world of gambling, horseflesh and adrenaline.

Antonio had once been a serious contender for international-level polo, but that had been before Michael Steele's actions had all but destroyed his family. Biting back the familiar anger that was never far away from his thoughts of the man, Antonio forced his attention back to the proposition.

'Can she do it?' he asked.

Dimitri shrugged, but Danyl seemed to be giving it some thought.

'Most likely,' he eventually said.

'I'm in,' Antonio stated with an innately Italian shrug of his shoulders. If Mason McAulty managed it, the win would be incredible. If she failed... Well, was there any such thing as bad press? Antonio liked the edge that it would place them on. Hell, he practically *lived* on it.

'Why not?' Dimitri said, throwing his hat into the ring.

Danyl nodded almost reluctantly, his lips a grim line of determination. Antonio might not know the source of the furious look Danyl cast towards the exit Mason

Mcaulty had left through, but he very much hoped she knew that she was playing with fire.

'Whisky?' Dimitri queried as Antonio finally took his seat.

'Absolutely,' Antonio replied, relaxing back and drinking in the sight of his friends. 'It's good to have you back.'

'Say that again and I'll *know* you've gone soft,' came Dimitri's terse reply.

'If I wanted to listen to a bunch of women gossip, I could have stayed at home and visited the harem,' Danyl concluded.

Antonio scoffed. 'You don't have a harem. If you did we'd never see you.'

But instead of relishing the familiar bond he had with his two closest friends, Antonio found his mind returning to the woman he had just decided to make his new PA.

Emma Guilham...

CHAPTER ONE

Eighteen months later...

EMMA SWEPT THE long tendrils of dark hair back from her face and into a discreet neat bun with swift efficiency. Even had she not seen Antonio Arcuri's occasional frown when a few strands would escape the hold these pins had on her hair, she instinctively knew that this was what her ruthless boss wanted from her. Discretion, speed and efficiency.

As she checked her appearance in the ladies' bathroom at the New York office of Arcuri Enterprises, the shadowed silver insignia of the letters *A* and *E* conjoined in the corner of each large mirror snagged her attention and sent a thrill of satisfaction through her.

She had come so far from her mother's small but comfortable home on the fringes of Hampstead Heath. She thought back to the quite outrageous way she had been interviewed by Antonio in that limousine, inching its way through London's Christmas traffic. She had, in her mind, been brazen. But then Emma had honestly thought that she stood no chance of getting the job. With nothing to lose and everything to gain, she had simply spoken the truth.

She had meant every word she'd said, and had stuck

to each and every one of them in the last eighteen months. She had fought so hard to be here—to be in New York, to be Antonio Arcuri's PA. And she wouldn't let his wholly uncharacteristic, unscheduled and increasingly imminent arrival now put her off her stride.

Ever since the ping had sounded on her phone at one in the morning, alerting her to the fact that Antonio would be back from Italy and in the office in less than six hours, Emma had felt something akin to panic. Only she had assured herself she no longer *did* panic. Instead, Emma had launched herself out of bed, scanned his appointments and found nothing in his diary to warrant such an unexpected return. So, she had no idea what to expect from her brooding Italian boss.

She had begun to look forward to the times when Antonio was away from the office. Whether it was for his immovable meetings with the other members of the Winners' Circle syndicate, or his visits to his offices in London, Hong Kong and Italy, she relished the time when she only had to deal with him through the separation of email and the occasional video conference. She welcomed these reprieves from his presence. Because in reality, in the flesh, Antonio was simply... overwhelming.

It was more than his classic good-looks. His bitter-chocolate-coloured eyes, set against defined cheekbones and a determined jaw would be devastating enough on any man. Along with the smooth Italian tan that contrasted with the deep rich wine colour of lips that were almost cruelly sensual. Every inch of him was honed, powerful and predatory. But she knew that even all those attributes combined didn't matter. It was the vitality—the authority that resonated from his very being—that really called to her.

But she had learned to temper her attraction. Refused to allow it to interfere with her work. She was here to do a job—not to lust after her attractive boss. She refused to fall into the trap so many other women had fallen into. Besides, she had goals—places she wanted to see, things she desperately wanted to do—none of which included Antonio Arcuri.

The door to the large office bathroom slammed open and a string of women rushed in, each armed to the hilt with make-up bags. Emma watched them for a moment, producing the tools of femininity that were used to enhance and seduce, delicately applying a million products as she once had, at the age of seventeen, using them with a heavy hand to mask the ravages of chemotherapy.

But she forced the memory aside. It wasn't as if Antonio cared at all about her appearance. Just her ability. Emma smiled ruefully at the row of Arcuri's female staff. Antonio had that effect on women. But not her. She might find her boss devastatingly attractive, but she wasn't going to be distracted by him.

She wasn't going to be distracted by any man.

Settled behind her computer in the outer room of Antonio's top-floor office, she let a feeling of control and calm wash over her. This was her domain and she loved it.

The clean chrome lines made the CEO's office on the twenty-fourth floor of the Manhattan skyscraper more than she could ever have imagined. The glass-fronted building afforded a highly sought-after vista of Central Park, allowing incredible views of the famous skyline to be her daily backdrop. The decor screamed money and wealth. Even if she only borrowed it during the day, before returning to her tiny apartment in Brooklyn each night.

Coming to New York had been the first thing Emma had been truly able to check off her Living List, after five years of remission had finally signalled the end of the terrible illness that had taken so much from her. And even if she had stayed in her role as Antonio's personal assistant for a little longer than she had originally intended, failing to tick off some of the other things on her Living List since coming here…she chose to ignore it. She was happy. And there was always time in the future—in *her* future.

'Do you know why he's here?'

Emma looked up from her desk to find James, a very nervous low-level exec, almost twitching with panic. He swept his glasses off his face, revealing bleary eyes, and cast her a look as other staff, equally nervous, watched from the corridor.

Word of Antonio's impending arrival must have spread like wildfire for, while it wasn't unusual to see *some* of the Arcuri staff beavering away at this ungodly hour of the morning, it was unusual to see *all* of them. But that was the effect of Antonio Arcuri. He didn't ask—he expected. He didn't demand—he simply didn't have to.

'Is he here yet?' James asked now, not waiting for an answer to his first question.

'Mr Arcuri has business to attend to, nothing more,' she said reassuringly, not really knowing if that was true or not.

'It's just that… Well, given the current climate…'

'Arcuri Enterprises is strong enough to survive *any* climate—current or otherwise,' Antonio's Italian-accented voice cut in harshly.

Emma hated the way he did that. Crept into rooms like a silent-footed panther. And she felt pity for poor James, who had turned from nervously pale to humiliated red with just one sentence from their boss, before fleeing the room.

Antonio turned on Emma. 'Why does everyone look as if they're about to get fired?' he demanded angrily.

Emma resisted the urge to sigh. He was clearly in *that* mood. A mood which made it easier for her to resist eating up the sight of his six-foot-plus powerful and lean frame.

'It is a little unusual for you to break your trip to Italy.'

'I need Danyl and Dimitri on a conference call immediately. And I need you to start a research file on Benjamin Bartlett. Everything and anything you can find on him and his company,' he said, throwing the last over his shoulder as he moved towards his office.

'I'll get the research team on it right away.'

'No,' Antonio said, pausing mid-stride. 'No one else is to know. I want you to handle it personally.'

With that, he stalked into his office, slamming the door behind him, and Emma sighed again. She closed the open folder on her desk concerning the Arcuri Foundation's charity gala—a project she had already invested much of her spare time in—knowing that she would have to take it home that evening. And as she dialled the numbers she knew by heart to get Dimitri and Danyl, she wondered just who Benjamin Bartlett was and why he was so important.

Antonio Arcuri willed the adrenaline coursing through his veins to subside. He discarded his suit jacket on the sofa and instead of taking a seat at his desk stalked towards the floor-to-ceiling windows fronting his office and flexed his hands.

He had decided to give the task of researching Benjamin Bartlett to Emma on the flight back here from his mother's house in Sorrento. He had been impressed with his calm, unflappable PA over the past eighteen months. Eighteen months in which he'd ruthlessly tamped down his initial and very much unwanted sensual interest in her from the moment she had stepped into the limousine on his way to the Asquith club in London.

Of course it helped that she dressed like the founding member of some religious organisation, and showed absolutely no interest in him whatsoever outside of their business interaction. He'd had PAs before who had raised their eyebrows and been uncomfortable handling some of his more indiscreet requests, such as fending off ex-lovers or acquiring suitable parting gifts. Despite what her conservative appearance suggested, Emma had handled each and every one without judgement or comment. The only thing she asked for was financial approval.

In short, Emma Guilham was *very* good at her job.

Which was exactly why he trusted her implicitly to handle the research on Bartlett. He couldn't risk news of his interest in the man leaking out before he'd had a chance to arrange a meeting with him. But it wasn't Bartlett himself that he was after. He could have taken or left his famous heritage brand, having no need to add it to his investment portfolio. No. It was the *other* potential investor that Antonio had in his sights. The investor that Antonio wanted to crush beneath his heel until no trace of him remained.

As he stood before the windows he didn't see a millimetre of the lush green sanctuary in the middle of New York's bustle. Antonio saw victory within his grasp.

Finally Antonio had the chance to bring Michael Steele to his knees. To cripple him completely, once and for all.

For so long he'd been nibbling away at the outskirts of Steele's business dealings. And each time Antonio took one more bite from the man's holdings he thought of his mother and sister. Of the shock and devastation Steele had wrought against his family with efficient ruthlessness. The subsequent pain that had nearly destroyed his mother, and the emotional scars that his young sister had turned against her own body until there had been almost nothing of her left.

Antonio had spent years clawing his way up the financial ladder...for this. The chance to destroy Michael Steele once and for all.

The buzz of the intercom cut through his thoughts and Emma's voice announced that she had Danyl and Dimitri on the line for him.

'What's wrong?' demanded Danyl.

Many would have been forgiven for thinking they heard anger in his voice, but Antonio knew better and identified concern.

'Nothing's wrong. In fact it's the exact opposite.'

'It must be...what?...six in the morning in New York?' queried Dimitri. 'Even *you* don't usually start until a bit later.'

'It's seven.'

'I feel sorry for your PA,' remarked Danyl. 'She just went into battle with my assistant to get me in on this call instead of calling the Terhren Secretary of State.'

'Don't feel sorry for her,' Antonio responded. 'Be impressed.'

'I am,' Danyl replied. 'Anyone who can put my assistant off state business is worth their weight in gold.'

'I have it. The way to take down Steele once and for all.'

Antonio didn't need to explain who he was talking about, nor why it was so important. Dimitri and Danyl knew what this meant to him—had meant ever since the age of sixteen.

'How?' asked Dimitri.

'I've been reliably informed that Benjamin Bartlett is looking for a healthy financial investment in his company. It would be Steele's last chance for financial security. He has the capital to invest, but not enough to survive without it.'

'And you plan to ensure that *you* win the investment,' stated Dimitri. 'Whatever you need—it's yours.'

Antonio smiled. 'That's not necessary. I can counter any investment offer he makes to Bartlett.'

'I've met Bartlett. I must say I'm surprised that he's looking for investment. He's always been financially stable.'

'You know him?' demanded Antonio. 'How?' he asked, his quick mind already working out how to use this to his advantage.

'He's a keen horseman. A regular feature on the international racing scene.'

Antonio frowned, scanning his usually perfect memory for any moment when he might have met the man amongst the numerous races they had attended as members of the Winners' Circle syndicate.

'He usually keeps to himself, though,' Danyl continued. 'Tends to stay away from the more *lively* areas that we enjoy. He'll probably be in Argentina for the first leg of the Hanley Cup. Do you know why he's looking for investment?'

'The why doesn't matter. I'll do anything to make sure that I win the investment and not Steele.'

Silence greeted his pronouncement. For a moment Antonio worried that the connection had been lost.

'Antonio, be careful. Desperation makes a man dangerous. I know this better than anyone,' Dimitri warned.

'I can handle the man.' Antonio practically growled down the phone.

'I wasn't talking about *him*.'

A knock on the door preceded Emma's appearance with the espresso he very much needed at that moment. Telling Dimitri and Danyl to hang on, he put the call on hold and waited for Emma to put the coffee on his desk and leave.

He was also buying time. Dimitri's warning hadn't fallen on deaf ears. But Antonio had spent years waiting for this day. He knew his mother would be saddened by his continued pursuit of revenge. She had pleaded with him over the years to move on. To put the hurt behind him—behind them all. But he couldn't.

As Emma retreated to her desk behind the door to his own office, he surprised himself by wondering if she would understand. There had been times when his usually conservative, cool-eyed assistant had shown a deeply hidden spark of defiance, something like the fight he felt at that moment. But as the door clicked closed he put that thought aside and resumed his call.

'That might not be the only problem that you face, Antonio,' said Danyl.

'Whatever it is, I can handle it.'

'I'm not so sure. Bartlett is notoriously moralistic. And your recent and very public exploits with a certain Swedish model might be a rather large putting off for him.'

An image of the blonde who had graced his bed for a number of months rushed into Antonio's mind. For the most part their encounter had run along the usual lines. Brief but sensually satisfying trysts whenever their diaries brought them together. Until she had started to ask for more. To ask for things he had told her wouldn't be part of their relationship. And when he had ended things she had quickly transitioned from a cool, poised and sophisticated companion into a raging, deeply resentful and incredibly publicly wounded lover.

'I can hardly be blamed for the fact she went to the press. I made her no promises—no lies were told. She knew the score and should have handled the end of our…interaction…with more finesse.'

'Whether or not she *should* have, she didn't. And Bartlett won't like it one bit. He has a strict morality clause for all his board members. And the last to break it two years ago is still looking for work, from what I hear.'

'What exactly are you saying, Danyl?'

'Well, you might need to take yourself off the market, so to speak.'

What? Shocked, Antonio didn't realise that the word had failed to escape his tightly clenched jaw.

'You've either shocked him into silence or you need to explain more clearly what you mean, Danyl,' Dimitri said, laughing.

'Marriage,' replied Danyl.

'Just because *you're* looking for a wife, it doesn't mean *I* have to.'

Everything within Antonio roared an absolute *no* at the idea. All the women he had encounters with knew the deal—even the Swedish model, though she'd seemed to forget it.

Short term, high hits of sensual pleasure were important to him. He was a virile male, after all, and not one to deny himself sexual satisfaction. But nothing more. He neither wanted nor needed the distraction of anything more permanent.

He washed away his distaste at the very idea of marriage with a hot, strong shot of espresso. He scanned his mind for any examples of a healthy, successful partnership and could not find one. Neither Dimitri nor Danyl had any particular fondness for the institution of marriage themselves, though for Danyl—being the future ruler of Terhren—it had become a considerably more pressing matter.

Their bachelor status was something that the press had latched on to more than once when covering the successes of their Winners' Circle racing syndicate. And it was certainly something that drew a wealth of beautiful women to their door. Was Antonio ready to consider closing that very door on the one thing aside from his business that he took *very* seriously?

'How bad is he really?' he asked his friends.

'That board member I mentioned…? He hadn't even had an affair. It was the rumour that Bartlett objected to.'

'Perhaps you don't have to…how do the Americans say it?…eat the whole hog—?'

'*Go*, Dimitri. It's *go* the whole hog,' interrupted Danyl.

'Please—we're talking about a wife, here. Can we leave out references to eating and hogs?'

'That's what I'm saying. Perhaps it doesn't have to be a wife.'

* * *

Emma had finished filing the quarterly reports, reassured countless staff members that, no, she didn't think Antonio's sudden appearance meant staffing cuts, and given consolatory smiles to a number of overly disappointed female employees who had failed to catch sight of Antonio before he'd locked himself in his office for most of the day. She had collated all the information she could on Benjamin Bartlett from initial online searches and saved it to Antonio's private drive, and finally settled down to eat the lunch she had missed three hours ago.

So, of course, as her mouth was full of avocado and bacon bagel, that was the precise moment Antonio Arcuri chose to appear before her desk. With a demand that took every ounce of her control not to choke on.

'Emma. I need you to find me a fiancée.'

Emma's usually focused and quick mind halted in its tracks. Of all the things she'd ever been asked by her notoriously difficult boss, this had to hit the top of the list.

'Do you have a particular person in mind? Or will anyone do?'

She had finally managed to swallow her mouthful around the shock that threatened to lock her throat in a seized position. And she was hopeful that her voice betrayed none of the sarcasm she felt so deeply, and instead projected only the smooth efficiency she knew Antonio prized so highly.

Emma loved being a personal assistant. She knew there were people who looked down on what they considered a lowly position. But, to Emma, the satisfaction of ensuring that her boss's day—his *life*—ran without stumbling blocks was important to her. She liked feeling indispensable. She liked knowing that she was part of something much bigger than she could ever achieve on her own.

And she liked fixing things.

If she was honest, it was because she knew how awful it was *not* to be able to fix something for herself. How scary and frustrating it could be. Whether it had been her breast cancer or the subsequent breakdown of her parents' marriage, she had been devastated by the sheer helplessness that she had felt at the time. And, whilst Emma might not have been able to fix the damage to her parents' marriage in the past, she could certainly help find Antonio a fiancée in the present.

Antonio pinned her with a gaze that would have removed a certain amount of testosterone from many of his male employees and likely increased the pheromones in the female ones.

'Was that sarcasm?'

'No,' Emma assured him, hoping the painful blush staining her cheeks wouldn't give her away. 'I simply wondered if you had your sights set on someone specific.'

'No,' he replied, frowning.

'So…' She battled on through the oddness of the situation. 'Do you have any parameters for this search? Wealth, previous marital status, level of attractiveness…?' She was desperately thinking of a polite way to say *bra size* when she registered with some surprise Antonio's confusion. He clearly hadn't thought this through.

'Reputation. She must be scandal-free.'

Emma fought to contain the rather un-ladylike snort that tickled her nose. It sounded as if he were looking to buy a prize heifer with an up-to-date vaccination history. Which made her wonder, horrified for a moment, whether the poor woman in question might in fact be required to present a full medical history.

'And I need her within two days.'

'Antonio, I'm not Amazon Prime. I can't just produce a…*a fiancée*,' she whispered harshly, fearing that she might be overheard, or even accused of some kind of highly salacious 'procurement' for her boss. 'Perhaps if you could explain the…the context, it might be slightly easier for me to…to understand what's needed.'

She knew she was stumbling over her words but, given his current mood, she clearly had to choose them wisely.

'I am about to set up a meeting with Benjamin Bartlett, who is touting for investment in his company. A company in which *I* must be the sole investor. And, being a notoriously moral man, Bartlett might be reluctant to involve himself with Arcuri Enterprises given…' He trailed off, circling his hands in a typically Italian gesture.

'Given your recent experience with Inga the Swedish—?'

'I know what she was, Ms Guilham,' Antonio cut in.

'Quite. So you need a beard?'

Antonio's hand went to the smooth planes of his chiselled jaw. 'A beard?'

'Not that kind of beard,' she said, suppressing the smile that toyed at the edges of her mouth. 'You need a fake fiancée to mask your previous indiscretions so that Bartlett will find you more palatable and therefore be more likely to welcome your investment.'

'In a nutshell, yes.'

'And am I to presume that all of this—' she said mirrored his Italian gesture '—needs to be kept under wraps? No one is to know about this, as well as the research into Bartlett?'

He nodded his dark-haired head once. 'There is another party interested in investing with Bartlett. My interest cannot get out to that person—or any other for that matter.'

The darkness of the warning in his voice was something that Emma hadn't yet encountered in her boss. And that in itself was enough to inform her that this wasn't to be taken lightly.

Her quick mind filed the top-line notes of his request. 'Okay. I'm going to need to clear your schedule tomorrow evening.'

This was why Emma was good, Antonio thought to himself. Apart from the slight slip-up of her earlier sarcasm, which he would happily put down to surprise, when she took on a task she was efficient, direct and held none of the self-doubt he had seen in staff twice her age.

He knew her announcement of his change of plan for tomorrow would be wholly and one hundred per cent in line with her new-found task. A task that she hadn't balked at, and had only posed pertinent questions on. Mostly.

'Done.'

'I'll have your blue tuxedo sent to the dry cleaners and prepared for the gala.'

'What gala?' Antonio queried.

'The Arcuri Foundation's yearly charity gala. You are usually in Italy during these two weeks, which is why you are never sent an invitation.'

'We have a charity gala?'

For the first time in eighteen months Antonio was

surprised to see something like anger in Emma Guilham's eyes.

'Yes, we do.' She paused, once again masking her obvious feelings on the matter with her legendarily cool gaze. 'And it will be the perfect place for you to find a fiancée.'

CHAPTER TWO

ANTONIO HAD SPENT the last twenty-four hours going over the research files Emma had put together on Bartlett—and the other research she had provided.

If he found anything distasteful about looking at the pictures and brief biographies Emma had collated of several of the single female attendees of that evening's event, he ruthlessly forced it aside. He had but one goal. And tonight would be the first step in achieving it.

Emma buzzed on the intercom, interrupting his thoughts to announce that the car was there to take them to The Langsford Hotel. Although it was only a fifteen-minute walk from the office, and he'd been inclined to make that walk, Emma had swiftly denounced the idea, saying that it wouldn't 'do' to have the CEO of Arcuri Enterprises *walking* up to the red carpet in front of the world's press. After all, she had said, she was apparently now in the business of safeguarding his reputation.

He'd repressed a smile. He was beginning to enjoy these brief glimpses of a dry English humour that she had hidden from him until now. Pulling at the sleeves of the tuxedo's jacket to fit them to the lines of his arms and torso, he opened the door to his office—and stopped.

Emma was perched on the end of her desk, leaning over towards the phone and looking quite unlike any way he'd seen look before.

She was still adorned in her usual monotone colours of black and white, and the wide panels of her loose dress covered all but the faintest glimpses of her figure. But her dark hair was piled up on her head in thick twirls, revealing strands of gold and deep reds that he had not seen before. It framed her heart-shaped face perfectly, and a light dusting of make-up served to accentuate the hazel and green of her eyes. A nude gloss lent a sheen to her lips that sent a punch to his gut more powerful than any brighter, richer colour could have achieved.

She looked natural and fresh—and so very different from the women he usually spent his time with.

'Yes, don't worry. The waiters know what to do. But because Ms Cherie was a last-minute addition to the invitation list we couldn't have known her dietary requirements before. The kitchen staff always make three extra portions of each main, so just reassure her that a vegan option will be made available to her.'

Antonio watched as Emma hung up the phone, catching the unusual sight of a long, shapely, creamy calf.

'Vegan?'

Emma turned, clearly surprised to find him standing there.

'Enough of a crime to scratch her off the fiancée list?' she asked.

'Not yet,' Antonio said, forcing his libido under control.

During the day—in her usual office attire—she wasn't so much of a problem. But even though Emma was covered from head to toe, that glimpse of smooth marble-like skin was enough to snare his attention. And he suddenly understood why Victorian England had deemed ankles the most threatening thing to society since smallpox.

Shaking his head to rid his mind of inappropriate thoughts about his PA, he led the way to the elevator that would take them down to the limousine waiting for them in the underground car park.

In the confines of the metal box, with Emma beside him, Antonio realised that it was going to be a long night.

Emma couldn't wait for this night to be over. They hadn't even arrived at the gala and she was already exhausted. It had taken every waking minute she'd had, not only to put together her research on Bartlett and compile the dossiers on Antonio's prospective fiancées—not that most of them *knew* they were prospective fiancées—but also to ensure that the foundation's gala wasn't single-handedly ruined by the very man in charge of organising it in the first place.

Marcus Greenfeld was a fusty old man, with fusty old ideas about how to run a charity. And it made her mad. She'd caught sight of his opening speech on the photocopier on the twenty-third floor and realised that something had to be done.

She'd hastily rewritten the thing, told a bold-faced lie to Greenfeld's assistant that Antonio had wanted to take a look at it, and sent it off to the teleprompter before Greenfeld had even been able to think of questioning it. Or question the three extra invitations she'd had issued to fiancée options four, five and six.

Antonio might have told her what he needed in a fiancée but, honestly, the man's taste in women was so

varied she couldn't tell which way he would go. Though
option two—the vegan Ella Cherie—was looking increasingly less likely.

As the limo pulled up to The Langsford she remembered she had yet to tell Antonio about the other last-
minute invitation.

'Dimitri will be here tonight,' she said as they slowed
to a stop. 'Danyl was...unable to attend.'

'Well, he *is* running a country.'

Emma wasn't so sure. She'd heard angry words in
the background when she was on the phone to his assistant. There had been something behind the bitterly
shouted phrase, *'I wouldn't go back to that hotel if you
paid me!'* that had made Emma concerned that her suggested location for the gala might be a mistake.

But there was nothing online other than praise for
this exquisite, world-renowned hotel. A hotel she'd
heard of even back in London, when she'd scoured the
press reports of its grand opening. She might never be
able to afford to stay in the amazing hotel herself, but
that didn't mean that she couldn't experience it vicari-
ously through work.

'Why?' Antonio asked, and Emma wondered briefly
if she'd missed something.

'Why, what?'

'Why did you invite them?'

'I thought that you might need some independent
advice on your choice.'

Antonio looked at her, but she was unable to divine
his thoughts.

'Wingmen—I thought you might need wingmen,'
she clarified.

'Emma,' he said, with censure heavy on his tongue.
'I have *never* needed a wingman.'

And the answering shivers that rippled through her body told her just how right he was.

As she did at most events Antonio attended for work, Emma stayed discreetly behind him during the initial introductions, her quietly whispered words prompting him with the names of the gala's guests and their partners. There had been times in the past when the additional information she provided had saved him from embarrassment—especially once when Antonio had nearly mistaken a man's mistress for his wife.

He was surprised to see so many recognisable faces. He could honestly say that he had never given this gala a first thought, let alone a second. If it didn't contribute to bringing Michael Steele down, it didn't matter to him. Marcus Greenfeld—the man Antonio had inherited along with the foundation he had secured for Arcuri Enterprises all those years ago—had never demanded anything of him and he liked it that way. Antonio had never taken to the man.

'Natasha.'

Emma's voice cut through his thoughts. He turned to find her welcoming the statuesque and considerably beautiful black woman making her way towards him.

'How lovely to see you again,' Emma said, kissing the woman on both cheeks.

The answering smile spoke of a friendship between the two and he instantly recognised the woman as fiancée option number one.

'Natasha—allow me to introduce you to Antonio Arcuri. Antonio—Natasha Eddings,' she said, gently proffering the woman to him like a gift, before swiftly disappearing to leave him alone with her.

Within minutes Antonio didn't have to bring to mind

Emma's handwritten scrawl on her brief bio—*This is my favourite*—to see why Natasha was Emma's choice. Natasha was articulate and intelligent, beautiful and, in short, practically perfect. But while she might meet *his* requirements, he had the odd impression that he did not meet hers.

'It would seem that my usual and widely reported charm might be falling a little flat this evening,' he remarked, testing his theory.

Natasha smiled apologetically. 'I'm sorry, Mr Arcuri. Emma did explain to me the delicate nature of your...interest,' she said, clearly searching for suitable phrasing.

A shiver of alarm passed through him quickly, but she pressed on.

'I assure you that I don't know why—only that you are looking for a fiancée—and no one will hear about it from me. I know that Emma has not spoken to anyone else of it. But...'

'You are perhaps involved with someone?' he offered, giving Natasha a way out.

'I am. Whoever you choose will be a lucky woman. I am sure of it. But I'm afraid I am not she.' Natasha smiled gently, smoothing any potentially ruffled feathers.

'Rest assured, Natasha, whoever he is,' he said, referring to her involvement, *'he* is the lucky one.'

The smile that lit her features was bright and spectacular.

'Thank you. May I offer a suggestion, Mr Arcuri?' When he nodded his assent, she continued.

'Perhaps you don't have to be looking so far afield.'

With that, she disappeared into the crowd, leaving Antonio with a thought that was matched only by a growing suspicion on his part. But the clinking of glass interrupted his partially formed idea, sounding out the fact that the opening speech from Marcus Greenfeld was about to begin.

Having prepared himself for the most boring fifteen minutes of his life, Antonio was faintly surprised at the warm, heartfelt introduction given by the man as he clearly outlined the charity's main functions. Though his voice was slightly stilted, the words were full of compassion and drive—and were, in a sense, a call to arms.

Looking across the audience, he saw them resonate, and a ripple of emotion shuddered through each of the attendees that he, himself, was not immune to. The only thing preventing the speech from being truly inspirational was the man delivering it.

From the corner of his eye Antonio saw his CFO, David Grant, approach quietly, and they greeted each other with a fond nod of welcome.

'I have to say,' Antonio said in hushed tones, 'Greenfeld's doing much better than I remember.'

His CFO frowned, then smiled. 'Ah… I heard that it was down to you, but now I'm beginning to think that your PA has been sprinkling her magic fairy dust over his speech—as well as over this gala.'

Antonio was confused. What had Emma to do with all this?

David let out a gruff laugh. 'For the last two months Emma has been running interference with Greenfeld and doing everything possible to ensure this night is an unusual success. You're always out of the country for this event, but it's been growing steadily more boring and more dull each year. It was Emma's decision to move the gala to The Langsford and provide gift packages for the guests. Not to mention rewriting the speech. She's done wonders.'

Wonders, indeed. Antonio was about to voice his frustration at the fact that his perfect PA had effectively been moonlighting, but David's next words stopped him short.

'I suppose it's only natural, given her personal experience. Cancer research is one of the main focuses of the Arcuri Foundation, and that clearly makes her the perfect support for the event.'

Antonio stared at his CFO. Cancer? Emma had experienced cancer?

A roar sounded in his ears and it took him a moment to realise that it was the sound of the guests applauding.

Emma had watched Greenfeld's speech from the sidelines of the large entertainment suite at the top of The Langsford. She had pretended to be checking the gala's gift bags, ensuring that the male and female packages were all present and contained the small bottles of champagne a local winery had been happy to supply. Other companies had also lent their support, through handmade bracelets and perfume for the women, aftershave and cufflinks for the men.

She knew she'd thrown Antonio's name around as if it was currency, but it had been worth it. And if her boss took issue with it, then she would set him straight. Tonight the gala was predicted to raise more money in donations than the last two events put together.

Once again she was pushing something bigger than herself out into the world, and this time she could do some actual good. Funding would reach beyond the not so small world of Arcuri Enterprises and help people— *really* help people who desperately needed it. And for that…? Yes, for that she would go into battle with her boss if needed.

But as her hands had hovered over the blue and pink cloth gift bags Greenfeld's voice had projected her own words back to her, and she'd cursed the man for not being moved, for the barrier between his words and the emotions she felt in her chest. The man was simply not good enough at his job.

Still, Emma chided herself, she couldn't do *everything*. Tonight she should really be checking on how Antonio was getting on in his search.

Although she was pleased with the fiancée options she'd miraculously pulled from the gala at the last minute, she had noticed Natasha's departure from her conversation with Antonio with something horribly like relief. She liked Natasha. The bright, intelligent woman had been at several of the foundation's functions, but hadn't been able to help the awful sting of jealousy curling in her chest as she had seen them talk.

Antonio might be an unconscionable playboy, and she might have had to smooth the emotional waters for his ex-lovers, but she'd never had to see it personally. Through the hackneyed words of the international press that followed him almost constantly, she'd been able to see simply an incredibly attractive man who enjoyed beautiful women with good grace and no false promises.

And if she was foolish to wonder what it would be like to be one of those beautiful women, then that was her own look-out.

She had long given up on fantasies of being a beautiful blushing woman on the arm of a dashingly handsome man. Her experience with cancer had seen to that. It may have stolen her breasts—which she had been prepared for. But somehow it had been the prospect of nipple reconstruction that had truly defined its effect on her sense of self. Unwilling and emotionally unable to face yet another surgery, Emma had instead opted for medical tattoos. The tattooist had been kind and had worked wonders. The tattoos meant that she didn't look in the mirror and immediately see something missing. The implants she could handle, and the scars she could deal with, but that last thing had been the hardest.

And, beyond the fight she'd won against cancer, it wasn't just flesh and time that it had taken from her. It had stolen her parents' marriage, and it had stolen her sense of femininity. At seventeen she'd been a child, and now, at twenty-three, she had yet to feel like a woman. She was unable and unwilling to put herself out there and find someone she might trust her delicate sense of self to—trust, should the worst happen, that they'd be there for her on the other side.

Her eyes were drawn to Antonio's presence across the room. Standing almost a foot above most of the guests, he was never hard to find. And as she saw him laughing with fiancée option number four—one of the last-minute additions she had added just in case—she gave herself a little mental slap.

Putting her feelings back into a box, she went to check on the preparations for the gala meal.

Had anything ever been as annoying to him as this woman's laugh? *Ever?*

Antonio couldn't help but think not, as she pealed out another reel of hysteria at an inane observation that had fallen flat on his own ears.

He couldn't hold it against Emma. Amber—he couldn't keep thinking of her as option four—was fine. On paper. Two degrees...a board member at her mother's make-up company...daughter of an international diplomat. Tick, tick, tick. But in person...? She was a car crash. She was loud, there was that awful laugh, and then there was her appearance. Clearly she was a stunning woman, but as she nearly fell out of her tightly constricting dress he couldn't bring himself to feel anything other than distaste.

'So, you're into horseflesh? I love to have a flutter on the ponies occasionally. You're going to be in Buenos Aires for the first leg of the Hanley Cup next week?'

His noncommittal 'mmm' wasn't enough to put her off. But it did remind him of the need to check in with John—the trainer he had secured for the Winners' Circle from the staff his family had been forced to let go.

It had been both a gift and a curse to work with the gruff northern Englishman. Antonio was still unable to relinquish fully the stranglehold the past had on him even now, in the present. He wondered if Mason McAulty was still furiously adhering to the strict schedule she had set herself...

But his train of thought was interrupted as Amber placed a long-nailed hand on his forearm, and Antonio resisted the urge to flinch.

'Is it true that you have a *female* jockey riding your horse? How simply thrilling!'

Cue more laughter. Laughter that made him wonder what dry response Emma would have come up with.

Damn it.

Emma—the woman he had worked with for eighteen months and never known about her medical history. He wasn't so uncouth as to require one for members of his staff, and neither was he such an ass that he would have treated her any differently. But as his eyes raked over Amber and her figure-hugging outfit he suddenly realised what it was about Emma's figure that had always niggled at the back of his subconscious.

Breast implants. He hadn't initially noticed them—in fact had only just realised that they *were* implants. They weren't obvious—in reality they were incredibly subtle—and the disguising of them was clearly intended by her choice of wardrobe.

In an act of what could only be described as self-preservation, any time he had come near to considering his PA's *assets*, he had swerved sharply away. So, even as a man who considered himself a connoisseur of beautiful forms, perhaps he could be forgiven.

Assimilating this new information about Emma didn't make him think any less of her—only more. It added yet another layer of complexity to a woman who was beginning to take up far too much of his thoughts for a member of his staff.

'And that was when—'

'I'm sorry,' Antonio said insincerely, 'I've just seen someone I need to speak to.'

He left the blonde woman practically stamping her foot in his wake and went to find... Anything would be better than that.

Until he walked smack-bang into Marcus Greenfeld.

'Mr Arcuri,' he proclaimed, before Antonio could extricate himself from the situation. The man took off his greasy glasses and began rubbing them with his tie. 'Kind of you to come. Didn't have to, of course,' he said apologetically. 'I hope you don't mind the...the extravagance. But then, of course, it was your suggestion so, yes... Thank you. I—'

'You have done an amazing job.' The lie was giving the man far more credit than he was clearly due, but it was necessary to ensure that Emma's inspired intervention was fully felt. 'This evening's gala has garnered a huge amount of positivity,' he said, loudly enough for Emma to hear as she made her way over to the two of them.

Did he notice a slight blush on her cheeks?

'Mr Greenfeld… Mr Arcuri—the meal will be served shortly,' Emma informed them.

Antonio's hawk-like gaze raked over her—*all* of her. Even dressed in the clothes he now saw that she wore like armour, she outshone Amber like the north star.

'I was just telling Marcus how much I'm enjoying the gala. A truly wonderful event. And with that in mind I have decided to double the donations raised this evening. Marcus,' he said, turning back to the man, 'please be so good as to announce that before the meal starts. Let's see if it greases some wheels.' He tried not to look at the man's glasses as he spoke.

His statement signalled the end of the conversation, but Marcus Greenfeld still took an awkward moment to realise it was his cue to leave.

Emma was looking at him with huge round eyes. The same eyes that had first caught his attention in London. He needed to get his own eyes off his PA and on to the next fiancée option. He needed to keep his mind on track. He wasn't here for the charity—he was here to help secure the Bartlett deal.

'That's…that's wonderful, Antonio. Thank you so much.'

'You don't have to thank me. It's my charity, after all. Besides… It's good publicity.'

'I don't believe that,' she said, levelling him with a stare that saw far too much, and speaking in a voice that held too much optimism. 'I think you're doing it out of the kindness of your heart.'

'Don't paint any illusions about me, Emma. Trust me—there's very little good left in me.'

'Well, then. I'll just have to nurture that last little bit of goodness.'

As she slipped away into the throng of guests his errant mind wondered what else she might nurture and he cursed himself to hell and back.

When the guests started to make their way in a somewhat chaotic line through to where the meal was being served, he saw Dimitri peel off from a group of attractive women.

'Enjoying yourself?' Antonio asked as they stood back and watched the guests pile in for the meal.

'Absolutely. I wouldn't have missed this for the world,' Dimitri replied, full of laughter.

'I'm glad you find humour in this.'

'And in your purpose,' Dimitri responded, clinking his glass of champagne against Antonio's. 'So, anyone caught your eye yet?'

As Antonio scanned the guests at the gala, all decked in the kind of finery that suited their opulent surroundings, his eyes snagged on Emma once again.

'Emma shared the list of suitable candidates with me, and I must say, apart from that girl Amber, she's chosen wisely. Though if you're not overly taken with option one I'd be happy to take her off your hands.'

'*Che palle*, Dimitri.' Antonio cast Dimitri a dark look, but his friend only shrugged.

'*Ti?*' Dimitri queried in Greek.

'Natasha Eddings—"option one"—is not up for grabs. This isn't a cattle market, Dimitri. This is important. If Bartlett is even going to meet with me, then I need a fiancée to resolve any detrimental effects of my previous…assignations.'

'Is that what the kids are calling it these days?'

'Don't joke. This is a serious matter.'

'I know,' Dimitri said, his eyes shining with understanding. 'But, Antonio, you can't just stumble across a woman you've never met before, make her an offer to be your fake fiancée, expect her to have little or no ulterior expectations, and present her to Bartlett wrapped in a bow.'

Antonio bit back a curse. Dimitri was right. Urgency and necessity had made his usually quick and clever mind sluggish and slow. He saw the many flaws in his plan immediately.

What had he been thinking? He needed the deal, he needed to bring Steele to his knees, and he needed a fiancée who would understand and support him in it.

His eyes caught Emma, laughing with a member of the hotel's staff before stepping away through the glass doors to the balcony that wrapped around the outside of the hotel. She had done so much. He was impressed with how she'd multi-tasked, clearly making an unprecedented success of the event whilst never missing a beat in her day-to-day role. She was conscientious, bright and articulate. And above all she was professional. In short, she was perfect.

'Mum, it's...' Emma paused, pulling her mobile briefly away from her ear to check the screen for the time '... one a.m. in London. What are you doing up?'

'Oh, I got stuck into a painting and the next thing I knew it was midnight.'

As Emma looked out onto the famous New York skyline she imagined her mother in the brightly lit, airy loft of her home in Hampstead Heath. When her parents had divorced her father had been the one to leave, moving into a flat nearer to the school where he worked, but only round the corner from the home they had all once shared.

The divorce had signalled the end of the nightly fights that had become a regular feature of Emma's life—desperate and painful arguments her parents had thought she hadn't heard. The heart-wrenching accusations, the arguments over how differently to handle their sick daughter, and her father's confusion as to why Louise Guilham had changed beyond his recognition.

Emma had initially felt relief when they'd separated, and then guilt, knowing that her father still desperately loved her mother. His painful bewilderment at the transformation in his wife and child had cut Emma deeply, and prompted the awful thought that had it not been for her illness her mother might have somehow stayed with her husband, and she might have somehow found a way to keep them all together.

'Where's Mark?'

Emma liked her mum's partner. He made her happy, and he also gave her the space she needed to be creative at unsociable times. Emma knew better than most that when her mum 'got stuck into a painting' she could be gone for days. She loved her mum's paintings—her favourite one hung on the wall of her little Brooklyn flat—and still felt bad that her mother's work had been put on hold during her illness at a critical time in her mother's career.

'Asleep. I just wanted to know how the gala went.'

'It's still going, but it's going well. Antonio has offered to double the event's donations.'

'That's wonderful, darling.'

But even through her mother's happiness for her Emma could sense her distraction. She was proba-

bly staring at the painting critically right at that very
moment.

Emma was about to ask when they might come over
to visit her. Her mother and Mark hadn't made it out
there yet, but that was okay, because she'd hardly had
a spare moment since working for Antonio. But as if
the very thought of him had conjured him from thin
air, she felt rather than heard his presence behind her.

'Love you lots, but I'd better go.'

Emma hung up the call and put her mobile back in
her purse. She gathered herself, knowing that her emotions were a little too close to the surface for her to face
her boss just yet.

Adjusting her mind's eye back from her home in
Hampstead to the beautiful night-time vista of famous
skyscrapers silhouetted against the stars, she felt a cool
breeze pass over her skin—and that was why she had
goosebumps, Emma assured herself. Not because Antonio had come out here to find her.

He should be with the other guests sitting down for
the meal. Perhaps he'd come to tell her that he'd found
his perfect fiancée, she thought, uncharacteristically
bitter.

She needed to pull herself together. Surely she could
handle Antonio Arcuri's fiancée as well as she could
handle him. But the thought of *handling* her boss gave
rise to some very explicit images, and she had to push
them aside as firmly as she placed a smile on her face
and finally turned to see him.

He stood half in shadow, peering at her through bitter-chocolate-coloured eyes. There was something about
the way he held himself. As if his body was restraining
some kind of pressing energy. Energy she felt all the
way on the other side of the balcony.

'Who was that?'

'What?'

'Who was on the phone that you love?' he asked, his Italian accent thick on the words.

Emma frowned at the personal nature of this conversation. She and Antonio didn't do personal. It was one of the things she liked and respected about him, and in her deepest heart she was thankful for it.

'My mother.'

'So there's no one at home waiting up for you? No boyfriend or otherwise?'

'No,' she replied, still confused.

'Then, Emma, I can see only one option before me. In order to secure the Bartlett deal I need *you*... *You* will be my fiancée.'

CHAPTER THREE

Huh... So *that* was what it was like to be proposed to.

It wasn't exactly how Emma had imagined it happening. Not even in her wildest imaginings. Though, if she was honest, Antonio Arcuri might have featured in some of her more fevered dreams—but never with such shocking words.

'In order to secure the Bartlett deal...'

'You will be my fiancée.'

While she might not have foreseen marriage in her future, if it *had* been to happen she would at least have hoped to be *asked*.

But why had he chosen her? Especially when he had a whole room full of perfectly suitable potential fiancées who were probably now picking the carbohydrates out of an exquisite three-course meal prepared by one of the finest chefs in New York.

She looked at him through the night gloom and saw something in his eyes. Something she had to look away from before it was transformed into pity.

'Who told you?'

'Who told me what?'

'Don't play games with me, Antonio. I'm not stupid.'

Anger ripped through her at an impossible speed. She'd wanted to start over. Start afresh in New York—

where people didn't know, didn't look at her as if she was an unexploded bomb waiting to go off. Yes, her work with the charity had naturally led to some astute observations by a colleague or two. But not Antonio. Because he hadn't known about her work with the charity.

'Is this because you feel sorry for me?'

'No!' he growled.

'I won't be used as some PR stunt to get what you want, Antonio. Playing on the sympathies of Bartlett with my "miraculous survival".'

'*Dio*, what kind of man do you take me for?' he demanded, clearly offended by the implication.

'The kind of man who would go to extreme lengths to acquire the perfect fake fiancée in order to pin down a business deal.'

'Well, I can hardly refute that claim. But my decision has nothing to do with your health and everything to do with the fact that you are a highly accomplished, educated woman who can move within my circles both with and without notice when necessary,' he stated, ticking her qualities off on each of his long, lean fingers. 'And, most importantly, you know that this will be solely a business arrangement. You will have no illusions of emotional investment that other women may mistake my offer to contain.'

'No, I don't have any illusions about the emotional investment behind your *"offer"*,' Emma replied, refusing to remove the sting from her tone.

Struggling to sort through the barrage of contrasting opinions he had bombarded her with, and against the wave of impatience he was sending her way, she turned out to the balcony.

He wanted *her* as his fiancée?

'I'm satisfied that you will not develop feelings for me and I will not develop feelings for you.'

A small sliver of hope curled in on itself deep within her. She should be pleased to hear that. She should want their relationship to be completely devoid of any possible emotional attachment, but somehow it still hurt.

'Why is this so important to you, Antonio?' she asked, hurt driving her to question her boss in a way she had never done before. 'You don't need the financial security of making the Bartlett investment, and you've never once cared about your…colourful reputation before. And surely if you want this deal badly enough you'll find a way to win against this other potential investor. What's really going on?'

He stared at her and said nothing for a moment. But then he spoke, as if realising that her agreement relied on full disclosure—or even part disclosure—and his next words shocked her.

'As I said before, it is not Bartlett that's important. It is the other man who might make investment in his company. Michael Steele is an evil man who cannot be allowed to succeed.'

Emma recognised the name, and knew that he had been the motivation behind some of Antonio's business dealings before.

'Why is Steele so important? Why go to such extreme lengths for a man who…?' She trailed off, not quite knowing who he was.

'A man who destroyed my mother and my sister's happiness—who changed their lives irrevocably and cruelly. This is Steele's last and final chance to gain financial security for himself. If he fails to win the Bartlett investment deal, he will lose his business. And I am determined to make that happen to the man…' He stopped, reluctance and anger warring for supremacy in his features. 'The man who is my father.'

Shock rippled across her skin and shivered through her body. Michael Steele was Antonio's father?

Antonio never talked about his family—had always valued his privacy above all else. She'd never once heard him mention his father—whose name he clearly no longer bore. But the darkness in his eyes and tone held so much anger and fury it crashed against her, pulled and pushed her away from Antonio like a tide.

It was unquestionable. And she couldn't help but wonder just how much his hatred of his father—something she simply couldn't comprehend—had driven him to this point.

'I will do anything to secure that investment, Emma. Anything. So if you have a price, name it. I will give it to you on a silver platter should you require it.'

Antonio would find himself a fiancée—whether it was her or someone else. But perhaps she could do something good with his offer. The thought raised hopes in her—some that she had discovered recently and some that she had long forgotten.

'What I want is for you to get rid of Marcus Greenfeld,' she practically growled. 'The man is incompetent and the foundation could be doing so much more. *You* could be doing so much more.'

'Is that it?' he demanded, his sensual mouth forming in a grim line of determination.

'Well, while we're at it, you can give each of my parents an all-inclusive holiday to wherever they want.'

'Done and done,' Antonio said, discarding her outrageous request as if it were nothing. 'You should know that as my fiancée you will be coming to Argentina for the Hanley Cup, once my meeting with Bartlett has been arranged.'

A rush of excitement swept across her skin. She'd always wanted to see the world. It was why she'd come to New York eighteen months ago.

'There will be a need to keep up this façade for a short while after the deal. Six months should be enough. So naturally you will accompany me on my visit to Hong Kong as well.'

As she thought through the future, to the trip to Buenos Aires and the trip to Hong Kong, the reality of what she was agreeing to dawned on her.

'And what about after Hong Kong? After six months when I'm no longer needed as your...your fake fiancée?'

'You'll be taken care of,' he announced.

She was sure he meant that. There was clearly no way she would be able to continue as his assistant once their 'engagement' was broken. She knew that he would provide her with a glowing reference and help secure her a future position, because he was that kind of boss. But she also knew—more than most—that the only person who could take care of her was herself.

No, she had never seen marriage or relationships in her future, but that didn't matter. Antonio wasn't offering her either. But there was something that scared her a little about being cut loose from her role as his assistant. And that, Emma realised, was the true price of what he was asking—her job. She had always meant to use this position as a stepping stone to other things. And maybe this was the not so gentle nudge that she needed.

Perhaps she could find work in Hong Kong? For a man she didn't find so frustratingly attractive. The trip to Argentina would be exciting too, and posing as his fiancée would be a way to help give her parents something too. Marcus Greenfeld would be removed and someone infinitely better, would replace him.

So, yes. Emma was prepared to cut her ties to Antonio once this was done.

'All I want is an appropriate reference.'

'Naturally,' he stated, as if they hadn't just bartered over the rules of their engagement.

Perhaps as his fiancée she would be able to tick off a few more things from her Living List. But she couldn't bring herself to ask for anything specifically for herself. After what she had faced, everything was a bonus. She didn't need anything more. Not really. The only thing she had ever wanted—could ever want—was for her body to feel like hers again. But not even the all-powerful Antonio Arcuri could do that.

'You have yourself a fiancée, Mr Arcuri.'

Finally, for the first time since Antonio had discovered that his father was after an investment in Bartlett's business, he felt the first taste of success on his tongue. Now all he had to do was get Bartlett to agree to a sit-down in Argentina.

His quick mind had already calculated the steps needed to accomplish that. But first he needed to reveal his new fiancée to the world.

He would, he realised, have to find a new PA. And, of course, ensure that Emma would have her pick when it came to choosing her next position. It was a thought that registered merely as an irritation alongside the satisfaction that Emma would be his. No, not *his*, he hastily affirmed. His pretend fiancée. For a business deal. Nothing more. He wouldn't risk *anything* interfering with his ultimate goal.

Another cool breeze brushed past them on the balcony and Emma shivered. He shrugged out of his jacket and placed it around her delicate shoulders. She accepted it without a word, clearly focused on her sudden and surprising 'promotion'.

Knowing they had to return to the gala, Antonio guided her through the balcony doors to the reception room. Even the dim event lighting was harsh on his eyes as they adjusted from the dark starlit night.

At the end of the room the doors were open and the gala guests were beginning to wander back through to the bar to continue with the night's agenda, hopefully having lined their stomachs in order to allow them to further enjoy themselves.

He judged that nearly thirty people were now filling the bar area, and decided that it would be enough.

'We should get ready to leave,' he said to Emma.

'The gala isn't set to finish for another two hours yet. I—'

'You can let the foundation's staff handle the rest. From what I've heard you've handled quite enough already. Besides, I have a feeling you're going to want to make a quick exit.'

'Why?'

He didn't give her time to think about it. He didn't give himself time to think about it. He had already decided his course of action should she say yes out on the balcony. He was about to ensure that the world knew about his new fiancée—in the quickest, most expedient way.

Antonio pulled her towards him, slipping his arms through the space between his jacket and her body. His hands met the curves he'd imagined to be there—the dip of her small waist, the arch of her back. They had a mind of their own as they swept across the silken material of her dress, sparking little bursts of electricity across his skin from the gentle friction. And his lips…

Emma felt the swift, determined crush of Antonio's mouth against hers. The shock of his hands against her waist, her back, startled a gasp from her. His tongue made swift work of the opportunity and plunged between her slightly parted lips.

Fire. Everything he did, every move he made, conjured up only that one word and that one sensation. It felt as if flames were licking across her skin, burning her from the outside in. For a shocking moment she thought her knees might buckle, and thrust out her hands to clutch the material of his shirt in her fists, anchoring them together even further.

As his tongue plunged more deeply into her mouth she felt as if her skin was a barrier—to him, to it, to what she wanted…

And then she heard the whistles. The cheers and the shouts grew louder, until she pulled back from Antonio's embrace and discovered they had a rather interested audience.

If Antonio had still been wearing his jacket she would have tried to hide in its lapels. She wanted the ground to swallow her up.

Until she realised that this public display was exactly what Antonio had wanted.

The stinging blush of embarrassment and shame painting her cheeks prickled and hurt. Of course he hadn't got carried away in the moment like she had. He had intended this. Was experienced in this. Antonio needed this and he needed her to play the part of doting fiancée—not naïve, out-of-her-depth PA.

She saw Dimitri come to the front of the crowd and

watched as a brief look of surprise was replaced with a surprisingly boyish grin.

'Permit me to be the first to congratulate you on your *now public* engagement,' Dimitri announced loudly, encouraging the already jubilant crowd into more cries of excitement and congratulation.

Within seconds mobile phone flashes were dusting them as if in strobe lighting. Antonio anchored her in place, pressed against his chest, smiling for all the world as if he were a newly engaged happy man, and Emma did her best to follow his lead.

After a minute Dimitri stepped forward to shake hands with Antonio, whispering that he hoped they both knew what they were doing through a fixed smile.

'Antonio is a very lucky man, Emma. But he is also a handful. So if you find yourself in need, you just call me.'

Dimitri pressed a kiss to Emma's cheek, and she couldn't help but smile back.

'Thank you, Mr Kyriakou.'

'Dimitri. Please,' he said, dipping his head low and studying her intently.

He didn't look at her in the way other men had once, but in a way that conveyed sincerity. And something slightly darker than his apparent good humour.

'I mean it, Emma. Anything. Just call.'

'Okay—that's enough. I don't need you putting off my fiancée at the very first step, thank you,' Antonio interrupted, with the kind of patience and affection only borne out of a long friendship.

'So,' Dimitri said, stepping back and rubbing his hands together. 'Would you like an impromptu engagement party? Or a highly skilful distraction so you can make a quick getaway?'

'A distraction, please, Dimitri. But nothing—'

'Nothing scandalous. Yeah, I got the memo,' he said with an eye-roll, disappearing into the crowd, calling for champagne and a dance with the most beautiful woman present in the room—aside from Emma, of course!

Antonio guided his assistant to the elevators, hoping that the kiss hadn't dulled her unflappable nature in the same way it had his. *Dio*, had he known that beneath that buttoned-up conservatively dressed professional there was a siren waiting to be unleashed, he might have given a second thought to making Emma his. His *fake fiancée*, an internal voice shouted in his mind.

He would have to keep such displays of public affection to a minimum if he were going to have a hope in hell of containing this situation. So he clung to the next step. Clung to what he knew needed to happen.

'Your passport. Is it still in the office?'

For a moment he thought she might not have heard, but then understanding dawned across her features.

'Yes.'

'And the change of clothes you usually keep there?'

'Yes,' she said, and her efficient swift nod did nothing to dislodge her perfectly placed hair, pinned at the base of her neck. His fingers wanted to reach out and pull that hair apart, feel it against his skin.

He forced himself to focus. 'Given the likely content of tomorrow's newspapers, and the public reaction to our announcement, it might be better if you do not return home this evening.'

Emma frowned, thinking through the suggestion. 'You think they know where I live? But I'm no one. How would they—?'

'You are not *no one*, Emma. You are now the soon-to-be Mrs Arcuri, and I don't think I need to remind you of the interest my considerable wealth brings.'

'And you wouldn't want a camp of reporters outside a tiny one-bed apartment in the deepest depths of Brooklyn?' she asked, with a trace of that British wry humour dancing across her words.

'I am not a snob, Emma.' He swung round to look at her, shocked that she might even think so until he saw the smile painting her pretty features as she turned her head up to his.

'Not going for the Prince and the Pauper angle?'

'I couldn't if I wanted to, Emma. I'm no prince, and I pay you considerably more than what a pauper has.'

Emma let out a huff of laughter as the lift doors opened onto the exquisite chequered foyer of The Langsford. She followed in Antonio's wake as they approached the reception desk. The words *penthouse suite* and *charge to my personal account* drifted through her mind as she watched the interaction, feeling oddly displaced.

It took her a moment to realise that he was organising for her to stay here, in this hotel. She was his assistant, the booking of hotels was usually her domain, and yet it felt… She couldn't find a word for what it felt like to see Antonio in action, catering to *her* needs.

As he led her away from the hustle of the concierge's desk towards a private elevator and presented her with a gold key card, he asked if there was anything she might need from her apartment. Anything that couldn't be purchased for her between now and Buenos Aires. There was no way he would let her go back to her apartment and deal with the gang of wolves that would be sure to be camped out on her doorstep, waiting for an interview.

Assuring him that there wasn't anything, Emma

stepped into the elevator and stopped. Antonio was staying in the foyer. He would either be going home or back to the office, she realised. She felt that she should say something, that there should be some conclusion to the events that had just happened, but oddly she couldn't.

'I'll need you in the office tomorrow morning, to pick up your laptop and passport and amend our travel details before we fly to Argentina.'

She agreed just before the elevator doors closed and she was taken upwards through the building. The smooth, swift motion seeming to increase the swirling in her stomach. What on earth had she just agreed to?

ARCURI OFF THE MARKET FOR GOOD?
BY ROANNA KING

Shock engagement of international
tycoon breaks hearts!

Female socialites around the world woke to breaking hearts this morning at the news that international investment tycoon Antonio Arcuri of Arcuri Enterprises is officially off the market.

The notorious and now presumably ex-playboy, often seen wining and dining a bevy of beauties from models to heiresses, has been stolen from our clutches by...his secretary!

Little is known of the Englishwoman Emma Guilham, other than that she has been in his employ for eighteen months and that she has been unavailable for comment.

Such a surprising turn of events must surely form a suspicion that there will be another shock announcement in just nine months' time. But,

*whatever the future holds for the happy couple,
this intrepid reporter is very much looking forward to what is sure to be the future Mrs Arcuri's
grand unveiling in Buenos Aires!*

Antonio had known the press fall-out would be big,
but Roanna King and her regular exposés on the private
lives of the rich and famous had made his engagement
sound torrid. That she had put the word *secretary* in
italics was bad enough, but the presumption that Emma
might be pregnant?

Antonio threw the newspaper across the small table
before him in disgust.

He checked his watch. His private jet had taken off
from a New York airport less than forty-five minutes
ago. Glancing across the narrow cabin now, he observed
Emma taking in the lavish decor of the Arcuri jet, and
hoped that it hadn't turned her head. She needed to be
ready for the call with Bartlett.

A thought which reminded him of the last phone call
he'd received on his almost constantly vibrating mobile
since the news of his engagement had broken.

No, he'd assured his mother, his PA was *not* pregnant.
Yes, he was sorry that he hadn't called to tell her himself. *Dio*, he cursed himself, he hadn't even thought to
warn her, to tell her. He'd been so focused on Bartlett
and his father that he hadn't realised how his engagement would look to his mother and sister.

As to his mother's question about when she might
meet her future daughter-in-law, he'd only been able to
put her off. *Would* they meet? he asked himself. He had
no doubt that the two women would get along fine. More
than fine, if he thought about it. His mother would appreciate the smooth efficiency and dry humour of the

small brunette. But it sat awkwardly with him, and he couldn't stop the words that Emma had said earlier that day about her own parents from ringing in his mind. *"I won't lie to them."*

She had been forced by the newspapers to contact her mother and father and explain the situation. He didn't like it—he didn't want anything jeopardising this deal—but he hadn't been able to refuse her request.

His own mother was a sentimental woman, who believed that love and happiness were a vital part of life and should be a vital part of her son's life. But he couldn't bring himself tell her that he had no room for such things. So, he'd lied to his mother and ignored the clenching in his gut. It was a sacrifice worth making, he assured himself, as finally Benjamin Bartlett had agreed to a phone call.

He had twenty minutes. Twenty minutes to convince Bartlett to come for a sit-down in Buenos Aires. Or all this would have been for nothing. Rather than allowing doubts to enter his mind, he should be using that driving force to push him forward. He would succeed. He had to.

Emma could feel impatience and expectation pouring from Antonio in waves. She tried to block it out and instead focus on the very strange and really quite wonderful experience of travelling in the company's private jet.

The limousine had taken them to the airport where, instead of queueing to get through Customs and Security, they had simply been looked over and then led up a set of stairs beside the plane.

Emma feared she might have been spoiled for ever.

She had ignored the way that the air stewardess had cast a disparaging look her way, seeming to take in her appearance and discard it as beneath her notice. It wasn't exactly Emma's fault that she was wearing yesterday's office clothes, having been unable to get back to her apartment and not yet having had the opportunity to buy new ones.

Still, she'd accepted the glass of chilled Prosecco the unnervingly beautiful woman had placed on the table in front of her.

The stewardess was clearly reserving her blood-red lipstick smiles for Antonio. Perhaps it was because of the article. She could hardly have missed the headline screaming about Emma and Antonio's shocking engagement on the newspaper beside the man in question. Not that it seemed to prevent the woman's bright gaze lingering on him as if she would like to consume him whole. Nor had it prevented the way her hand rested on his shoulder just a little bit too long to be appropriate.

Emma cursed the way her stomach dropped as she wondered whether they had perhaps enjoyed each other's company before. Jealousy wasn't part of their bargain and she wouldn't let it dim the fizz of excitement that was building as she adjusted to the realisation that they were actually going to Argentina.

Her Living List might be full of hopes and dreams, but they had been practically based on her income, on her finances. This deal with Antonio took her possibilities to a whole new level. As his PA she had only ever borrowed a taste of that elegance, but now she could experience it for herself. Perhaps for these six months she could enjoy all that Antonio had to offer. Well. Almost all. She knew she wouldn't have the one thing that her body refused to realise she *couldn't* have.

Antonio's phone started to vibrate noisily.

'I'm going to put it on speaker,' he said, leaving the

phone to jerk around on the table between them, as if this wasn't the one phone call he'd been waiting a week to receive. 'I'd like your opinion on Bartlett, given your research.'

She nodded, and he finally accepted the call.

'Mr Arcuri?' Bartlett's assistant was on the line.

'Yes.'

'Mr Bartlett for you. Hold, please.'

The line went silent for a moment.

'Arcuri! I hear congratulations are in order…'

Antonio froze at the American's cultured tones; for a second they had sounded so much like his father's. He muted the call momentarily, cleared his throat and then resumed the call, cursing at the fact that Emma had witnessed this errant chink in his defences.

'Thank you, Mr Bartlett, your congratulations are very welcome.'

'Am I to presume that your insistence to speak to me is down to the fact that you have uncovered the news that I am looking for investment?'

'Yes.'

'Then I would love to know your source. I was under the impression that it was a highly guarded secret.'

'A gentleman does not kiss and tell, Mr Bartlett.'

'I would hope that you have been kissing no one other than your fiancée, Mr Arcuri.'

'I assure you that is most definitely the case,' he said, trying to ignore the way Emma was watching him. 'As to how this information was uncovered—I assure you that it was not from any party related to *your* business.'

Antonio knew there was enough weight in his tone to indicate that the leak had come from the only other person involved in the negotiations. His father. It was exactly as Antonio had intended.

'I must say I am surprised,' Bartlett pressed, refusing to rise to the bait, 'that a man such as yourself—a man with a reputation for ruthlessness—would want to invest in *my* business.'

'You have a quite remarkable heritage brand, Mr Bartlett, one that any investor would be lucky to be involved with. And ever since I began my relationship with Emma I have been motivated to make more…holistic business decisions.'

'Your relationship is quite recent?'

'Emma has been with me for eighteen months, and during that time I have come to realise what a wonderful woman she is,' he said, this time unable *not* to look at the woman in question—unable to take his eyes from the faint blush that rose to her cheeks. 'She is kind, caring and compassionate, Mr Bartlett, and I am sure you will discover that yourself, should you choose to meet in Buenos Aires and discuss things further.'

There was a pause on the line.

'As you are aware that I am looking for investment, I am sure you are also aware that your father is the only other petitioner in the matter?'

'Surely whether I am aware or not is incidental? Having two people determined to win investment into your company can only be a good thing for you.'

'I appreciate that, Mr Arcuri, but I refuse to allow this to turn into a circus. I have my reasons for wanting to keep this investment opportunity quiet, and if I am to meet with you in Buenos Aires then I want your assurance that it will remain the case.'

'I promise you, Mr Bartlett, that no one will hear about this matter from me, or anyone connected with me.'

'Good. Then I look forward to meeting both you and

Ms Guilham in Argentina. But I warn you, Antonio, your father's offer is good. You'll have to do something pretty spectacular to rival it.'

Antonio let Bartlett's warning settle in his mind as he finished the call. He gathered his thoughts, and was curious as to what Emma had taken away from the conversation.

'So…?'

'I think you are going to have to work hard to win his approval,' she replied grimly.

Bartlett's warning was irrelevant, he told himself. Antonio had waited sixteen years for this. Sixteen years to take his father down for destroying his home and his family.

He would do *whatever* it took to ensure it.

CHAPTER FOUR

EMMA WAS ROUSED from her sleep as the limousine pulled up to The Excelsus hotel in Buenos Aires and she wished she had managed to stay awake. The view from the plane as it had descended into Argentina had promised a stunning and wonderful place that she'd only ever had an internet connection to. Having booked Antonio's travel itinerary there a number of times, Emma had been eager to see it for herself.

She'd been captivated by the tall, gleaming structures that reached into the sky, surrounded by a harbour of sand and sea, with twinkling with promise and excitement in the morning light, and she was sad that she had slept through the journey the waiting limousine had taken once they had made their way through the sleek airport hallways.

As she got out of the car, surprising both the driver and Antonio—clearly she had been expected to wait for the door to be opened for her—she was hit by an almost cold wind, the kind that she had come to expect from an English autumn. Remembering that Argentina's coldest winter months took place during June and August, the slight chill in the air made Emma nostalgic for home.

When Antonio failed to emerge from the car, she turned back to catch his gaze through the open door.

'I'm going on to the stables. You can go on in and rest up in our rooms if you like.'

But Emma didn't want to go to the hotel. She wanted to see Buenos Aires—wanted to see the grand entrance to the race course and the small lakes she had only seen in internet pictures.

'I'd like to see the stables,' she said, but the slight delay in the careless shrug of his response made her realise that she was imposing. That he might want this time to himself.

'By all means,' he said, gesturing her to return to the car.

She got back into the warm interior, thankful for the heat that softened the surprising chill still stinging her arms. The fresh air had wiped away the jetlag she hadn't so far been aware of. Having stayed awake during most of the flight, she had effectively worked through the night and arrived in Argentina late morning, with only two hours' time difference.

She settled back into the plush leather seat, desperately trying to ignore the proximity to her boss that shouldn't be affecting her the way it did.

Antonio's fierce gaze was locked on the scene outside the window, as if he was actively trying to ignore her presence. But he had agreed that she could accompany him to the stables, and Antonio was not a man who would have agreed had he really not wanted her there, she assured herself.

The car took a sweeping loop away from The Excelsus, and Emma was slightly disappointed to find that it pulled up again only a short while later. The stables were housed directly beside the hotel, and she vaguely remembered that being the reason Antonio preferred to stay there.

This time she waited for the driver to open her door, and a half relieved, half satisfied look crossed the man's features. She thanked him and then stood up to take in the incredible view as he went to open Antonio's door.

The grounds of the racetrack were long and rectangular, flat and surrounded by thin fencing. Off to the left the impressive stretch of the hotel building loomed over the edges of the race course, with thin lines of aqua-blue hinting at the infinity pools that were boasted by the hotel. In her mind she filled in the hundreds and thousands of people who would cover the stands and the balconies on race day, and the incredible noise they must make.

She heard the slam of the car door behind her, and turned to see Antonio stalking off towards a group of large white buildings with terracotta-coloured roofs that reminded her oddly of the American stables she had seen amongst the Winners' Circle holdings. She followed him through the fenced-off area, where there were more signs of life, people and horses emerging from corners and shadows as if they had previously been hidden from view.

She was two steps behind Antonio as he went deeper and deeper into the large central building.

To call it a barn would be wrong. The sheer size of it could have enveloped the whole apartment block she lived in back in Brooklyn. This structure had sleek lines, all glistening steel and chrome, and the expansive concrete floor was spotless and wet from where a young teenager further down was cleaning it. The smell of horse sweat and manure was barely discernible, and the only sound she could make out aside from Antonio's leather-soled footsteps was a hushed conversation coming from one of the stalls.

* * *

Antonio was so conscious of Emma's presence he almost missed the broad sound of John's northern English accent coming from the stalls where Veranchetti was currently housed. At sixteen and a half hands, the horse was glorious. Its black coat gleamed in the shafts of sunlight filtering through the window at the back of the stall.

As he neared, the voices became more distinct, and the feminine lilt of an Australian accent came to a halt.

'Antonio?' John's voice called out from inside. 'That you? Reckoned you'd have swung by before now.'

Only John could make the reproach sound like a greeting. Antonio caught Mason's eye as she made her way out of the stall. A brief nod was all she threw at him before heading off out of the building.

'How are you?' John asked, coming out from the stable.

'Good, John. I'm good.'

'I'll say,' John observed, watching as Emma stayed just behind Antonio. 'I take it this is the lass, then?'

Antonio felt himself on unsteady ground as he suddenly realised that he had failed to take into account yet another person he now had to add to his list of deception. John was the only member of his father's staff he'd stayed in contact with after he, his mother and sister had been forced to return to Italy.

It was a contact that he and the other members of the Winners' Circle syndicate had very much used to their advantage.

'Must say, I would've thought I'd not have to hear about it on Twitter.'

'Since when are *you* on Twitter?' Antonio asked, a smile playing at the edges of his mouth. 'John—allow

me to introduce you to Emma Guilham, my fiancée.'
The word felt strange on his tongue.

Emma came forward, having hesitated only slightly
when he'd said *fiancée*. 'Nice to meet you, John,' she
said warmly, reaching out to shake his hand.

'Oh, no, lass, I'm all mucky,' he said, wiping straw
and mud onto his already dirty jeans.

'Don't be silly. I'd hardly be a match for Antonio Arcuri if I was worried about a little dirt.'

John let out a bark of laughter, shook Emma's hand
and turned to Antonio, his eyes approving. 'I'm going
to like her. First one I've met of yours—and the last,
by all accounts.'

Something like guilt threatened to spark in Antonio's
gut, but Antonio pushed it aside. *Dio*, he couldn't let
her anywhere near his sister Cici. His sister would be
broken-hearted when it all came to nothing.

'How's V?' he asked, swiftly changing the focus of
the conversation.

'Veranchetti,' replied John, 'is doing fine. Survived
the trip over and has been acclimatising for a good
while now.'

'And McAulty?' Antonio asked.

From what he'd heard in the last eighteen months
she'd been doing everything she'd said she would—living and breathing the horses from the Winners' Circle
stable. John had been giving him, Dimitri and Danyl
weekly reports, and had voiced his positive opinion
and utter confidence in her on more than one occasion.

'She'll do.'

It was about as high a seal of approval as John would
ever give. And, from the way he was looking at Emma,
it seemed to be covering both of the women who had unexpectedly entered Antonio's life in very different ways.

Antonio had felt the calm of being inside a stable settle over him from the moment he'd come out of the wintry sun and moved into the shadows. But it was an odd calm. It always had been. The kind of calm that happened before a storm was about to hit and change everything.

He wondered if it was like Pavlov's dog—if in some way he'd always feel like this in a stable. It was the one place where he'd repeatedly sought refuge when things at home had got too much. When he'd wanted to take the first horse he saw and ride like hell away from his home, his father and all that entailed. It was the kind of calm that anticipated adrenalin…anticipated action and adventure.

It was the kind of calm he hadn't felt since being forced away from his home, his horses, and his once possible career as an international polo player.

As if John sensed the dark memories taking hold of Antonio, he led them from the quiet peace of the stable back out into the sunlight.

'Were the overnighters okay?' Antonio asked. It would have taken them a long time to get from America to Argentina, with several stops along the way.

'Yep—paperwork was all in place, and everything went well. You might want to check in with the folks from the Hanley Cup. They've got some things for you to sign.' John indicated over his shoulder to where there was a small office hidden amongst the larger buildings.

Antonio nodded his head, willingly taking the proffered escape from the stables and the threatening memories of his past.

Emma didn't know what she'd expected from the stables, but it hadn't been John. In the eighteen months she'd worked for Antonio she'd never had anything to do with the Winners' Circle. He'd handled all that himself. Oh, she'd been curious—but never enough to intrude on Antonio's personal endeavours.

John had watched Antonio walk off towards the office and now turned his attention back to her.

'I've known that one for a long time, Emma.'

'Is this the bit where you warn me off?' she said, half joking and half afraid of what he might say.

'No, lass. Reckon you know what you're getting yourself into. But that boy…he's just like a natural-born mustang. Wild and ready to bolt at any moment.'

Emma wanted John to stop. She was struggling enough to maintain the image of Antonio as her boss and now her fiancée. She wasn't sure she was ready to see him as the boy he'd once been.

'His da,' John continued, 'he were a hard man—no doubt. And he all but broke that boy. You've got him this far, Emma. Hold on to him. Even if he tries to bolt. He's worth it, lass.'

She didn't know what to say. She couldn't tell him the truth. That this engagement of—what?—less than twenty-four hours?—was just for show. Just for a business deal. The sincerity ringing from John's voice was irrefutable.

She smiled, knowing that she couldn't do anything but keep up the façade and not break an old man's heart. 'I'll do that, John. Or I'll try,' she said on a laugh, to lighten the tone.

To change the subject, she nodded back towards the stable.

'Is Veranchetti the horse Mason's going to ride in the Hanley Cup? I'm afraid I don't know much about it,' she said ruefully.

'Yup. They've got good a chance, I reckon.'

'It's an odd name—though I suppose they all have odd names.'

'Cici—his sister—named him after the hero of one of her favourite romance novels. Antonio didn't have the heart to say no,' he said, squinting in the sunlight, looking out at the course.

'Does Cici ride?'

'No, she was never that interested in the horses. But you don't want me raking up old ghosts, Ms Guilham.'

Whether John had purposely shied away from the past, or whether he'd noticed Antonio's return, she couldn't tell. Either way, his presence clearly sounded the end of their conversation.

'John's been telling me that Veranchetti's chances are good. I might even have to place my first ever bet!' she said brightly.

Antonio's dark glance told her that he didn't believe her, and as he said his goodbyes and ushered her back towards the limousine Emma felt horribly as if she'd been treading where she shouldn't have been...

The foyer of The Excelsus gleamed in the sunlight through the glass-fronted entrance. She resisted the temptation to shiver, which was more from the incredible luxury surrounding her than the temperature. Her low heels clicked on the marble flooring as they made their way towards the reception desk.

'Mr Arcuri!' A perfectly suited manager greeted Antonio and then turned his attention to Emma. 'And Ms Guilham. Welcome to The Excelsus.'

Momentarily startled that the manager had greeted her by name, Emma was wrong-footed.

The man pressed a sleek black folder and two black-coloured room cards across the desk towards her. 'Your belongings have been taken up to the suite. Would you like me to show me to your rooms, Mr Arcuri?'

'No, thank you, I am sure that everything will be in order,' Antonio responded, pausing only to pick up the folder and key cards before marching towards a discreet lift hidden behind steel panelling in the opposite direction from the more public elevators in the centre of the foyer.

Emma was left trailing behind, feeling once again unsettled in this environment. The excitement she had felt back in New York when she'd stayed at The Langsford was beginning to rise again. This was a glimpse of a lifestyle, experiences, that she couldn't have imagined putting on her Living List, and she was eager to see her room.

As she came to a halt beside Antonio the question she'd felt niggling at the back of her mind had clearly become apparent.

'Yes?' Antonio demanded, with a return of the autocratic boss she knew he could be, who for just a moment had been absent at the stables.

'How did he...?'

'Know your name? I would think that, just like John, *many* people now know your name. After all, to all intents and purposes, you are the future Mrs Arcuri.'

Emma remembered the press articles speculating on who she was, how she had managed to capture the notorious playboy, whether she might be carrying his child. She was thankful that she had managed to get hold of both her parents to let them know what was about to happen, but hated to think of them reading all the gossip and conjecture.

The discreet lift doors opened and Antonio entered,

waiting for Emma to do the same—but she couldn't. He was in there, taking up the whole space, dominating it. Some kind of self-preservation instinct kicked in, preventing her from joining him. Until Antonio reached out a hand, caught her by the wrist and pulled her right into hell with him.

The move had startled her so much she had fallen against him, found herself pressed against the hard planes of his chest, and the physical contact drew an almost instantaneous reaction from Emma, who had been trying desperately to forget the shocking kiss that had announced their engagement to the world.

He was looking down at her, his dark hawk-like eyes watchful, almost waiting…

'Capable of standing on your own two feet?'

Embarrassment painted her cheeks red as she disengaged her body from his. The lift was ascending with barely a jolt, and she put the flip of her stomach down to the ascent of nearly twenty floors in just seconds.

Coming to a halt, the lift opened onto a hallway with only two doors at opposite ends, and Emma slapped down her active imagination that had been expecting to walk straight out into a penthouse suite.

Not waiting for her, Antonio exited and made his way towards the door to her left. She followed, and as he swiped the key card and pressed his way forward into the suite she hovered by the door.

'Emma?'

'Yes? Oh, sorry. Now that you're safely settled in, I'll take my key and find my room,' she said, trying to look anywhere but at where her new fiancé was standing.

His silence drew her gaze like nothing else could have. He stood there, barely a hair out of place despite the flight and the visit to the stables, his head cocked to one side, and looked at her with something in his eyes she didn't want to name.

'This is your room, Emma.'

Shock kept her in place, hovering outside the door to the suite. She was pretty sure her jaw had dropped.

'That's not going to work, Antonio.'

'Of course it is. You're my fiancée—where else would you be staying?'

'Who's to say that I'm not the kind of fiancée who believes in…in waiting for the wedding night?'

Words like *sex* were dangerous at the best of times, but with him…? She cursed internally. She wasn't going to be able to do this.

'No one—and I mean *no one*—would believe that I would allow my fiancée to have her own set of rooms. We're on this path, Emma, and I will not let anything or anyone question that. This is going to have to be believable, so get used to it.'

He was standing in front of her now, so close, and strangely even more dominating than he had been in the lift.

Before she could take a breath, he continued, 'You have your company credit card?'

Her mind was spinning enough that she was not able to understand why that would matter, but she nodded.

'Good—perhaps if you look the part it will help you act the doting fiancée.'

She looked down in dismay at the sensible, albeit rumpled clothes she had worn on the plane. He was right. Not only did she need a whole wardrobe of clothes—those she hadn't been able to retrieve from her apartment before coming here—but she needed a particular style of clothing.

She scowled at him. *'No one,'* she said, echoing his earlier words, 'would believe you would settle for *doting.'*

The concierge at The Excelsus had arranged for a car to take her to the most exclusive mall in Buenos Aires, with the assurance that it had a wide selection of fashion stores from which she would be able to get everything that she needed.

In the years since her breast reconstruction Emma had taken to shopping for clothes online, enjoying the fact that she didn't need to expose her insecurities to anyone but the four walls of her bedroom. This, however, was daunting. But she knew Antonio was right. The level of sheer extravagance in even the daywear of the women in the hotel had been enough to convince Emma that if she needed to be Antonio's fiancée, on his arm at evening events and at the racetrack, she would need thick and very expensive armour to succeed.

Besides, millions of women around the world who'd had reconstructive surgery did this every day. So could she.

But now, standing in the fourth store she'd entered, she felt the drive and determination that had brought her there beginning to fade. It wasn't just a dress or two that she needed—it was an entire wardrobe. She knew that there were women who would kill to be left free in one of Argentina's hottest fashion districts holding a credit card without a limit, but right now it was all just a little too much.

Some of the shocking and outlandish creations she had seen on display were so far outside her comfort zone, and the sheer sensuality of the Argentinian designs were both tempting and frightening in contrast to the office-style respectability of the clothing she was used to wearing in New York. But this was getting silly. She had spent so long hiding her figure behind loose clothes and dark colours. Perhaps this was a chance to make the most of this opportunity—even if she did feel slightly out of her depth.

She took her courage in both hands and approached a saleswoman who had been eying her suspiciously. Briefly, in a no-nonsense way, Emma explained the situation.

Rather than cloying mawkish sympathy she had prepared herself for, she was surprised and oddly touched when instead the woman beamed, informing her that she would be utterly delighted to help.

Antonio had just exited a shop, with a present each for his sister and mother safely in transit to his hotel, when he'd caught a glimpse of Emma slipping into a store. He'd held back a moment, losing her briefly as she moved amongst the mannequins and rows of designer clothes. Then, curious to see how she was getting on, he hadn't been able to help himself as he followed her in, telling himself that he only meant to make sure that she chose clothing suitable for her new role.

He'd felt the vulnerability coming off her in waves when he'd discussed her need for a wardrobe, and had had an urge to reach out and comfort, to protect. The only other women in his life he'd ever felt like that about were his sister and his mother, and from them he understood only too well how important it was for a woman to feel beautiful in what she wore.

As he neared the back of the shop he was surprised by a high-pitched *coo* falling from the lips of a shop assistant. He turned just in time to see Emma twisting around to catch a glimpse of herself in the floor-to-ceiling mirror by the changing rooms.

Need and desire consumed him fiercely and unexpectedly the moment his eyes snared her. There she stood, in a strapless dress that hugged her perfect breasts and stomach, leaving her arms and shoulders bare while layers and layers of blood-red silk cascaded from her slim waist, looking almost as shocked as he felt.

He watched as she took in her own appearance, her eyes drawing upwards from where the dress fell at her bare feet all the way to the top, where she met his eyes in the reflection of the mirror.

In a second the shock in her gaze was shuttered. Her eyes narrowed and she spun round, looking at him accusingly. 'How did you find me?'

Affronted by the way the fire in her voice matched the temperament of the dress, he couldn't help the retort that fell from his lips. 'I don't have a tracker on your phone, if that's what you're implying.'

She scowled, and oddly Antonio felt—and resisted—the urge to laugh.

'I'm here by mere coincidence,' he concluded.

'You don't believe in coincidence.'

'No,' he said, feeling exasperation rise within him.

He really didn't, and in that moment he wondered what kind of game the gods responsible for their lives were playing. Because that was exactly how he felt right now. *Played.*

As her hands clutched instinctively at the skirts of the dress he remembered just for a moment the feeling of her skin beneath his palms, and he forced himself to turn away before he embarrassed them both. The almost painful shock of arousal had hit him hard, and he knew it had nothing to do with how much time had passed since he'd last been in bed with a woman.

He could almost *taste* desire as he made his way over to the seat beside the dressing room. He was some kind of masochist to stay, but he didn't have the will-power to leave.

A glass of champagne was left discreetly on the table beside the chair, and when he took a sip the bubbles scraped against his raw throat.

'It's not right,' Emma said, looking at him, and for a moment he forgot that she was speaking about the dress.

He felt his eyes narrow instinctively, and everything male in him roared that she was wrong.

Before sanity prevailed.

'Perhaps not. Try something else.'

It was a command. Uttered in a harsh tone. One that did not befit the dressing room, and Emma felt it down to her very soul.

Yet she didn't think that they agreed for the same reason. She had never chosen clothes to accentuate her breasts before. At least not since the surgery. Before that she had been seventeen and happy with her body. Had never suffered from the kinds of insecurities she'd seen in her friends as they judged themselves against each other, against impossible to achieve celebrity figures.

But afterwards? Yes. She had let her insecurities run her wardrobe.

The selection of clothes given to her by the lovely sales assistant here was impeccable. Some of them were rather more extreme than others, but she had begun to view it as a kind of shock therapy. The more ex-treme made the less outrageous palatable, when once she would have baulked at the whole lot.

Emma had known women—powerful, strong, inspiring women—who had embraced their bodies and their lives with vigour after chemotherapy. She had longed to find that sense of self, and now she was beginning to realise that the courage that had seen her battle fiercely with the chemo was still needed to battle her future.

Stepping back into the changing room, she fought the instinctive urge to run. Run from Antonio's assessing gaze…run from the desire. She wasn't foolish enough to try and hide from what it was that had sprung forth between them.

She undid the zip hidden in the side seam of the dress and it pooled around her feet. She stepped out of the delicate red silk and her body felt the lick as if of flames across her body. There was only a thin curtain of material separating her from Antonio. She knew it and so did he.

Her exposed skin feeling overly sensitive, she reached for the last dress the assistant had procured for her.

Having already chosen some incredible day clothes, she only had evening functions to cater for, and she cursed herself for leaving the best for last. It was her favourite dress of the selection, and she'd wanted to have this moment for herself. But outside sat Antonio, glass in hand, as if he were waiting for a show. Except rather than taking her clothes off she was putting them on.

Suddenly she wanted him thrown off balance as much as she was. She wanted him to be feeling just an ounce of what he was doing to *her*.

Standing in a thong and nothing else, she reached for the dress and stepped into the skirt. The fabric of the dress's blue silk was covered in a subtle lace flower pattern detail, with a figure-hugging bodice. It rubbed against her sensitive skin at the same time as the cool silk soothed. The sleeves were sheer, with the same lace detail covering her arms but leaving her décolletage bare. It covered even whilst it revealed and she silently thanked the shop assistant's perfect eye.

Before she stepped out into the dressing area she looked at herself in the mirror, feeling that same sense of shock she had experienced when she'd seen herself in the red dress moments ago.

Was that really her? Whilst her hair and minimal make-up were almost ordinary, the dress had called forth something within her. Something powerful and feminine… Things she'd always wanted to be but had never seemed to achieve. There was a blush to her cheeks, making more of her cheekbones than she was used to, and the glitter in her eyes shone like diamonds.

She pulled aside the curtain that separated her from Antonio and everything else faded away—the assistant, the shop…it all disappeared and only he came into focus.

And her lungs stopped working.

Because Antonio Arcuri, destroyer and saviour of global companies, was looking at her as if she were the only thing in the world and she nearly came undone.

CHAPTER FIVE

THREE DAYS OF trying to ignore the woman living and breathing in the same suite was driving Antonio insane. He was now thoroughly regretting the impulse he'd had to stay and see Emma's last outfit at the shop. Ever since that moment he'd been imagining what it would be like to peel her out of the silky dress and enjoy every delight her stunning figure had to offer.

But he couldn't. Emma was nothing like the women who graced his bed. The women who lived and played in his world—the women who had the hard edge needed to take his emotion-free entanglements. Emma didn't know how to play that game, and although she might hide it well she would break in his arena.

Besides—as he reminded himself for the hundredth time—there was far too much at stake.

He had done everything needed to ensure the meeting with Bartlett would be a success. He had orchestrated an irresistible deal the man would be insane to refuse. But he didn't like the silence from his father. Didn't trust it. The man must be up to something.

For the first time Antonio found himself wondering just how far he would go to get his revenge.

And the only answer in his heart was, *However far it took*...

It was gone eleven, and Emma had retired to her room almost an hour ago. In that time he'd pulled out all the files on Bartlett they had collated in the last week and turned the sumptuous living room into a practical office. The meeting with Bartlett was set for tomorrow evening—and the day of races that would commence the first leg of the Hanley Cup would start the following morning. Everything was lining up nicely... But he couldn't shake the feeling of an approaching storm.

As if he had summoned demons for Emma too, he heard sounds of distress coming from her room. Worried, he got up from the sofa and was halfway towards her door when he heard her scream. He rushed into her room, barely noticing as the door slammed back against the wall, probably leaving a dent, and took three strides to her bed.

She was tossing and turning, caught up in the cotton sheets, kicking out desperately. He could see the trails of tears on her cheeks. *Dio*, it must be some nightmare.

Remembering how his sister had suffered so badly from them in the year following their departure from the States, he sat down on the bed beside Emma's restless form and gently took hold of her arm.

'Emma...' he whispered. 'Emma, it's just a dream.'

She thrashed against his gentle hold and let out a whimper that struck his heart.

'Emma, come on. It's just a dream. You need to wake up.'

Her eyes sprang open, searching for focus. A shudder racked her body, and she gasped on an inhalation of much needed breath.

'You're okay. It was just a dream.'

But the hurt in her eyes told him he was wrong.

She looked so vulnerable, so in need of comfort, that

it took everything in him not to take her in his arms, to replace the fear in her eyes with want, with arousal. He wanted her to feel the same need, the same desire that burst into life against his skin when it met hers… something he knew could only be satiated by a touch, by a caress.

He cursed himself to hell and back. He couldn't take advantage of her. Not now…not like this. *Not ever*, he warned himself.

Emma took in Antonio's presence. The light filtering through from the living room cast his face in night-time shadows, so much more welcome than her awful dream. For a moment—just a moment—she thought he might reach for her. Might kiss her as she so desperately wanted to be kissed. But seconds passed and he didn't. He held himself back.

She nodded. Resting her hand on his where it held her arm. 'I'm okay. It's okay. I'll be through in a minute. I just need…a minute.'

As Antonio left her room she willed the fierce beating of her heart to slow. Her fingers brushed away the traces of the nightmare from her eyes and she realised that the tears she had thought contained by the dream had escaped.

She moved to the en suite bathroom, passing the wardrobe full of the clothes they had bought two days ago with an accusatory glance, as if they could be held responsible for causing old fears to surface. The fear that the cancer would come for her again, just when she was beginning to hope that she could reclaim her sense of self, reclaim the sense of her body.

She splashed water on her hot cheeks, finally shaking off the hold of her terror. Wide awake, and not ready even to consider going back to bed, she pulled on the hotel's silk robe and padded into the living area of the suite on bare feet.

She took in the devastation caused by Antonio's preparation for the meeting with Bartlett with a rueful smile.

'I am very glad you don't usually work like this. I'd have the cleaners quitting on me each and every day if you did.'

He looked up from the papers he held in his hands, his hawk-like gaze refusing to be distracted by her attempt at small talk.

'Nightmare?'

'Yes. Clearly,' she replied.

She was surprised to see his chiselled features soften.

'My sister used to get them regularly. Would you like some tea?'

'Because I'm English?' Emma asked, holding on to the warm offer like a lifeline.

'Yes. Clearly.'

She smiled as he gave her words back to her.

'What would you have given your sister?'

'Well...' he said, as if searching his memory. But she knew that the answer would immediately be on his lips. 'She was thirteen at the time, but a little limoncello didn't hurt her one bit. Not that this hotel has limoncello stocked in the suite's bar. But there is whisky?'

'I'll take the whisky. Thank you.'

As she watched him step behind the corner bar that edged one side of the suite she took in his powerful appearance. Even three days of solid work, constantly sorting through all the figures and research data that they'd been able to put together, hadn't put a dark hair out of place. Dressed in his suit trousers and a shirt, sleeves rolled back on strong tanned forearms, he was mouth-wateringly handsome.

The brief glimmer of concern in his eyes as he had woken her from her nightmare had been devastatingly tempting, and not for the first time Emma wondered what it would be like to rely on that power, that compassion. A compassion he was yet to show, however, in any of his business dealings.

She turned away from the temptation of his presence and stepped towards the windows that looked out over the stands of the race course. In just a few days they would be full of spectators, sound and chaos. But at that moment they seemed peaceful and quiet. She pressed her hand against the glass and allowed it to leach away some of the fevered heat she reluctantly attributed to the man behind her.

As he approached, a glass of whisky in each hand, she became horribly conscious that she was only wearing a silk negligée and the robe. The cool, delicate touch of the fabric did nothing to ease the prickles of heat racing across her skin at the mere sight of his reflection. Her mind, torn between the horror of her nightmare and the ecstasy of Antonio's proximity, warred between her hurt and her heart…

Her heart should know better. But it didn't. Her heart wanted him to put those damn glasses down and take her in his arms.

Schooling her features, calming the erratic beating of her pulse, she watched as he waited for her to turn, clearly knowing that she had seen him in the reflection in the window.

'My sister never really wanted to talk about her fears, but in the end she saw that it helped.'

Desperate to hold on to any thread that took her away

from her desires, and also curious, given how little she knew about his past and his family, she turned and accepted the glass he offered her.

He moved back to the beautiful sofa and cleared some of the paper from it, making room for her on the opposite end, a safe distance away from his presence.

'How long did she have nightmares for?'

For a brief moment Emma wondered if Antonio would choose to ignore her question, but after a small sigh he started to talk.

'They carried on for a year after my parents' divorce.'

His eyes turned dark, consuming the golden flecks she sometimes saw there.

'It was public and very messy. In order to reduce the settlement, my father paraded my mother's affair through the courts and the international press. He had the divorce granted in Italy, where people are still notoriously moralistic about such things. Had we been in North America, it might have been different. But whatever continent he might have chosen, it didn't seem to affect the press interest.'

He shrugged—such an Italian gesture of dismissiveness for clearly such a painful thing. Emma could only guess at the depths of the emotions he was struggling with.

'How old were you?'

'I was sixteen, but Cici was only thirteen. Without Michael's financial support my mother couldn't stay in America. Her father offered to help, but only if we came back to Italy. So we left.'

'That must have been hard.'

Emma knew what it was like to have her entire world change at such a young age. It had dripped onto her experiences like rain falling through leaves. Each tear-shaped drop hitting another aspect of her life. It could not have been much different for Antonio, his sister and his mother.

'It was. Everything we knew—friends, school, staff. That's where John worked. In my father's stable.'

'You had a *stable*?'

Emma had known that he must have had money growing up—he had some mannerisms that only financial security could give—but the idea of having a stable was almost inconceivable for a girl who'd had a struggling artist mother and a state school teacher father.

Antonio smiled ruefully. 'The full American package. Stables, private education, piano recitals—for Cici, not me. I was on track to be a member of the American polo team. But... I left that behind too.'

She let the silence fall, not wanting to interrupt the hold of his memories. Her heart reached out to the boy who had lost his dream.

'Cici struggled with it more. Losing her friends. And, even though he's an evil bastard, she suffered from the loss of her father too.'

Emma couldn't help but notice how he referred to his sister's pain, but not his own. *Her* father, not his. As if Antonio had cut him out of his vocabulary as determinedly as his father had cut them from his life.

She took a sip of her whisky. His was neat, but he'd added ice to hers which she was thankful for. The ice-cool liquid took the edge off the warmth of the rich Irish blend.

'Cici needed stability in that year, and I worked very hard to give it to her.'

'What about your mother?'

A small smile graced his lips. 'She was—*is*—a beautiful Italian socialite with little education and less work experience. Her father was rich, but bad financial investments had stolen much of his wealth by the time we returned to Italy. He gave us what he could, but I wanted Cici to stay in private education. In order to do that I needed to work after school.'

'And what about you?'

'I,' he said with mock sincerity, 'am an academic genius.'

And she wished he hadn't said it. The playful mask he wore was just as alluring as the truth behind it.

'I didn't need private education. I got my scholarship to NYU...met Dimitri and Danyl. They became my family, each of us having experienced our own hardships. There we were, foreign students, not unaccustomed to America, but perhaps our differences forged our friendship as much as our similarities. We worked hard and played harder. It was at university where we first conceived the Winners' Circle syndicate. My interest in horses had never faded and it was matched by Dimitri's and Danyl's. It was they, along with a small investment from my grandfather, who helped me start Arcuri Enterprises. Within two years I had paid them all back with interest, and bought my mother and sister a house—a *home*—in Italy. Dimitri and Danyl helped me ensure that they would be okay.'

'You protected them. Your sister and mother.'

She cursed her foolish heart for unfurling beneath the warmth of his words as he spoke of his friends, his family. And finally she began to understand Antonio's determination to secure the Bartlett deal. He wanted revenge—that much was clear. He wanted to hurt his father in the only way that he knew how.

But Emma couldn't help the feeling growing within

her that he might not like what he found once he'd achieved it.

'Yes,' he said simply, in relation to her earlier statement, as if it was the only way it could have been.

'It must have been a hard responsibility to bear,' Emma observed.

'I would do it again and again.'

'Where are they now?'

This time his smile broadened fully and her heart nearly stopped at the sight. It illuminated his dark features with light and pleasure, and in that moment she was thankful that he wasn't like this all the time. It would be...devastating.

'A beautiful estate in Sorrento, on the Amalfi coast, with olive trees and lemon groves.'

His simple words conjured a million images in her mind, and she could almost smell a hint of citrus in the air about them.

'And your sister?'

'No more nightmares.'

'Nothing more to fear,' Emma said, her own nerves beginning to twist at the way the conversation was going.

'No.'

'And what is *your* fear, Antonio?'

Emma didn't know what gave her the courage to ask. Perhaps it was the darkness outside, or the intimacy created by the only light in the living room dusting them with a warm, gentle golden glow.

But even in that soft lighting she saw his features grow dark. Something bitter entered the air, and the determination that had hung around Antonio since he'd come back to the New York office and asked her to research Benjamin Bartlett returned.

'That my father will never pay for what he did to my mother and sister.'

And for what he did to you, Emma added silently as the ripple of his words sent icy shivers through her body.

She took another sip of the cool whisky, trying to forestall the question she knew was next on Antonio's lips.

'And what is yours, Emma?'

Antonio watched Emma pull the thin silk robe around her shoulders, covering and protecting herself from the memory of her nightmare. He wished for a moment that she hadn't. The way the soft material had opened just slightly at the V of her chest, the smooth creamy skin thinly veiled, had been his only anchor—his only tie in the storm of emotions that had surfaced beneath his stark words as he'd recounted his past.

He heard the chink of ice in her glass, drawing him back to the present as she rested it between her palms as she might hold a hot drink.

'Well, I suppose the nightmare started in pretty much the usual way—I was being attacked by zombie cats.'

He couldn't help but laugh. 'Zombie cats is usual?'

'Well, hyper real, at least. They were attacking me, and I was managing to escape, but they were keeping me from something. And then I realised that they were keeping me from getting to a doctor's appointment. I was waiting for new test results.' She took a shaky breath. 'The cancer had come back.'

Shivers covered his forearms. He couldn't even begin to imagine that kind of fear. 'What was it like?'

'Horrible,' she said simply, without malice or anger, or any of the kind of emotions he would have projected onto the situation.

He wasn't sure about continuing to ask, but he felt that she needed to talk about it, and he trusted her enough to tell him to stop if he caused too much pain.

'How old were you when you got ill?'

'Seventeen.'

Antonio cursed. It fell from his mouth without thought or he would have held it back, but Emma only smiled her gentle small smile.

'What surprised me was how utterly practical it all was. The diagnosis was shocking, terrible, but there was a chain of events to follow—things to be done and so much to organise. After a few days the diagnosis became a fact. Just a fact. A hurdle—a thing to overcome. All the stress and worry about A levels, about boys, about who was better friends with who…the things that had seemed so important in my day-to-day life…suddenly just seemed so small in comparison.'

'Weren't you angry?' he asked.

'Yes…and no. There wasn't really time to be angry. There was the operation, and then the chemo. And through it all I just felt that I couldn't let the anger take hold. I felt that my anger would feed the cancer, some-how. It's so very different for each person it happens to. Some people are able to use anger to fight it, to give them energy. But I didn't want anything else eating away at me. If I clung to being positive, if I held to the determination that I would beat it, then I knew I would win. I would take back my life.'

She took a breath and he marvelled at her strength.

'I had to put my A levels on hold during the treat-ment. I had a double mastectomy, then chemotherapy followed by breast reconstruction. Some women choose to have the reconstruction immediately following a mas-tectomy, but after speaking to my doctors I wanted to make sure that the cancer was completely gone before moving forward. And at that point I really didn't want another operation.'

Antonio saw the fierceness in her gaze as she spoke. The fire he had only seen glimpses of before was there now, shining in her eyes, burning in flushed cheeks, and it was glorious. He relished her strength and determination, allowed it to feed him too.

'It took about a year, all in all. And by that time, although supportive, my friends had moved on…found relationships, started university, gone travelling around the world. None of which I begrudged for a second. But I felt out of step. Just a little behind. Like this thing had happened to me and no one else. But that wasn't quite true.'

'What do you mean?' he asked.

'One of the hardest things was telling other people. I felt as if I had to manage their emotions, their reactions. I'd find myself reassuring *them* that I would be okay. That it would all be fine. More often than not it was just—' she shrugged '—awkward.'

She took another sip of her drink and a little shiver rippled across her skin as she swallowed the oaky alcohol.

'I had a boyfriend at the time,' she revealed, swirling the ice cubes around her empty glass. 'He was a…a sweet boy. But I think telling him was the hardest. Because the look in his eyes…' She shook her head against the memory. 'It was fear, guilt, anger… Fear of what might happen, guilt that he didn't want this, that it wasn't what he'd signed up for, and anger that this had happened to him. Yes, clearly it was happening to me, but it was something that he might have to deal with.'

'He left you?' Antonio asked, hearing the growl vibrating in his own words. The sheer anger and fury swept up in him by her simple words shocked him.

'No. We'd only been dating—if you could even call it that—for a few months. It wasn't serious, and it probably wouldn't have lasted much longer. So I let him go. He argued with me. I could see that he wanted to do the right thing. But I needed to focus on me, on my fight, not on ensuring that he was okay.

'I was determined to ensure that the cancer cells didn't multiply and spread—didn't affect things outside of my body. It's so hard not to let cancer become everything around you. Everything you see. Family.... Friends. Cancer is a thief if you let it be. It doesn't just take lives, it takes body parts, time, experiences, relationships...

'My parents' marriage broke down soon after my treatment,' she confided. 'They're much happier now, and that's great. But nothing was the same after the cancer. My home, my parents...my body. Everything had changed.'

'I'm sorry.' Even as he said it, he knew the words to be inefficient, wrong...too little.

'Don't be sorry,' she said, a flash of anger sparking in her eyes. 'Don't apologise. Because cancer shouldn't be excused. It's not a thing to pardon or to forgive. It is not a thing to be normalised. You don't get to apologise for cancer. You can help fight it. Help beat it. Help those who *do* fight against it. But *never* apologise for it. There's funding for research and new technologies... that's why charity foundations are so important. That's why *yours* could be so much more.'

Antonio held the weight of her gaze, held the weight of her accusation. He knew she was right.

She seemed to gather herself before him. 'I'm sorry,' she said.

'Don't be. You're right. I should have been more involved. I should have made the time to attend the yearly galas. And you're absolutely right about getting rid of Greenfeld. I've already put motions in place that will remove him from his position. After the success of the gala—which was mainly down to you—the board supports my decision and we're already considering other options. Once this deal is done, I promise you it's the first thing on my list when we return to New York.'

Emma smiled—almost as if she had a secret.

'What?' he asked, suddenly incurably curious about her—everything and anything about her. He wanted to know it all.

'I have a list too.'

Emma couldn't believe that she was telling him about her list. During chemo she had heard people talk about their bucket lists, and had felt overwhelmingly sad that the supposition was at the end there would be death, not life.

'It's my Living List. My mum helped me to make it,' she said, smiling at the memory of being in her parents' sitting room, pen and paper in her hands, as her mother and father encouraged her to write down everything she wanted to do when it was all over.

'What's on the list?' he asked, drawing her from her memory.

She looked at him and realised how their bodies had shifted position on the sofa. Somehow during their conversation she had turned towards him, her back against the armrest, her legs stretched out. If she moved an inch her feet would be in his lap. And Antonio had turned

towards her, mirroring her position, one leg bent, anchored over the other.

It was beguiling, having Antonio Arcuri's full attention. The low light from the small lamp on the table beside him shaded half his features, highlighting the cut
of his cheekbones, the hollows of his throat…a throat
she wanted to run her fingers over, her tongue…

But it was the look in his eyes as he asked the question. Curiosity and something else. Something almost
pleasurable.

She felt heat swirl in her stomach and, desperate to
dampen this quickening attraction for her boss, she focused on his question.

'A whole lot of things—big and small.'

'What's the biggest?'

'Only a man would ask that first,' she joked, and
appreciated the humour that was returned to her in his
eyes. 'Okay—I think the biggest would be that I want
to see the sun rise over a desert and set over the Mediterranean.'

'In one day?' Antonio asked, his surprise almost
funny.

'Not necessarily. I'm not fussy. Just a sunrise. Just
a sunset. But, yes, deserts, sea views… I want to see
the world. I'm really looking forward to Hong Kong,'
she confided.

'I know the perfect place to take you.'

'Where?'

'It's a surprise. But you'll like it,' he assured her, and
that thrill of excitement began to unwind throughout her
body and across her skin. 'The smallest?' he pressed.

'Ah. The smallest I *have* achieved. I wanted to eat
a stack of American pancakes with crispy bacon and
maple syrup. It was *divine*.'

He laughed as she groaned with remembered pleasure. 'What else?'

And once again Emma's thoughts went to the one thing that she hadn't been able to write on the list in front of her parents. She was sure that her mother would have understood, but writing *losing my virginity* had just seemed more than a little uncomfortable.

But it was about so much more than simply having sex. At the time, Emma had been approaching her reconstructive surgery with the same practicality that had pushed her through the other areas of treatment.

Now, when she looked in the mirror she just saw shapes. The shapes that had been taken away and then put back on her body. It was hard for her to see her breasts, her body, as her own. To own them, to glory in them. She had a good figure—she knew that. But somehow she had never felt able to exalt in it. To see it as her *own*.

'You didn't ask me to help you achieve anything on your list,' Antonio stated when she didn't answer his question.

'When?'

'When I offered you whatever you wanted.'

'No,' she said. She hadn't. 'These are things *I* want to achieve Antonio. *I* want to make them happen. Asking you to do them for me…kind of feels like cheating.'

He let that lie between them, and the silence was consumed whole by the tension and crackle of attraction on the air between them.

Antonio's declaration to dedicate more time and energy to the charity had been almost fierce. And Emma found herself wondering what it would be like to have that dedication and power directed at her. As a woman. As someone or something beautiful.

She couldn't help but study him once again in the half-light of the room, seeing the way it illuminated his masculine beauty. She could lie to herself and pretend to think that it was her wayward thoughts about her virginity that had conjured her attraction to him by association—not the curve of his almost cruelly sensual lips, the feel of his eyes on her body. She could blame it on the new and surprising intimacy that had been created between them in these last few hours and not on the way his direct gaze, eagle-eyed and intense, seemed to reach into her and kick up her pulse.

But she wouldn't.

She had always found Antonio powerfully attractive. Had always felt prickles of awareness when he was nearby. He was as tempting as the devil.

Those gold flecks had returned to his eyes, surfing the waves of molten chocolate that seemed to radiate…heat. And desire. It became a tangible thing, and she could almost taste it on the air. She felt every single inch of her skin where the silk robe rested against it, felt the smooth material of the sofa beneath her calf muscle. She felt the space between them that seemed at once so small, yet almost insurmountable.

She willed her breath to become silent, knowing that she couldn't give in to the temptation burning between them, reluctant to let sound or action break this strange hold.

But sanity prevailed. Yes, she'd seen more to her handsome boss than she could have imagined. The grief and pain of his childhood had called to something within her. But she couldn't get involved with him. Because for all his promises she couldn't rely on anyone if the worst was to happen. Because it never lasted. Not really. People left, people changed, people wanted other things… And in the end the only person Emma could rely upon was herself.

She looked about the room, finally severing the connection that had formed between them. And then, lifting up a stack of papers, she asked him about Bartlett— a line of questioning that Antonio seemed equally relieved to take up.

'Bartlett's company is a fourth generation, family-owned heritage business and—'

'No, I didn't mean his company. Who is *he*? What makes him tick?'

Antonio paused for a moment, as if he honestly hadn't given it much consideration. He picked up the files and she shook her head, a gentle laugh falling from her lips.

'Antonio…' She couldn't help chuckling as she gently reprimanded him. 'He is the father of two children, Mandy and James, both are at university, both studying business. Mandy, by the way, certainly seems to be enjoying it thoroughly from her Instagram account—'

'You follow her Instagram account?'

'Yes, you asked me to research Bartlett, so I did.'

He nodded, as if slightly surprised. 'How did you get all this?'

'Bartlett's PA—Anna—used to work for someone who does a lot of business with the boss of your London office. We know each other quite well. She helped with some of the information, but she wouldn't cross any lines. Perhaps you should take a look at the notes in the blue folder. They're a bit more personal than business facts.'

But the word *personal* brought back memories of the earlier moment they had shared.

Realising that she had lost his concentration, Emma

felt a wave of tiredness sweep over her, and as Antonio took up several of the documents in the blue folder she decided to leave him to it and return to her room. This time hoping not to avoid her nightmares but dreams of her handsome boss.

CHAPTER SIX

THE NEXT DAY, by the time Antonio returned to the suite, he was physically exhausted. He'd been down to the stables to see John and V, but John had practically thrown him out because his 'state of mind' was affecting the horses. So he'd spent two hours in the gym, pushing himself hard.

Anything to force his shockingly one-track mind away from Emma Guilham and back to the meeting they had with Bartlett in a little over an hour. He had tried to pretend that the intimacy they'd shared the night before didn't mean anything. He'd tried to ignore the strands of desire that had woven between them before she had shifted the subject away from the personal and back on to Bartlett. But he hadn't quite managed to achieve it.

John was right. Antonio had to get his mind in order—had to shelve these thoughts and put them back in the box he never opened. He needed to get Bartlett to choose him, because if he didn't his father would go unchecked. Michael Steele would live his life without ever feeling what his mother felt...his sister felt. The painful sting of humiliation, the acute devastation when everything changed beyond recognition...the realisation that the very fabric of life could not be trusted.

And Antonio needed that—needed Michael to feel that.

He walked into his room and pulled his sweat-soaked T-shirt over his head, discarding it as he crossed into the bathroom. Turning on the scalding hot spray of water, he pushed the rest of his clothes from his body and tried very hard not to imagine Emma doing the same. Before she covered that irresistible body in the dress he'd bought for her that morning.

He hadn't been able to help himself. The clothing she'd purchased on their first day in Buenos Aires was perfectly adequate. But he didn't want 'adequate' for her. After last night, he wanted to see her in colours. Because that was what he had seen when she had talked about her experience with cancer.

He didn't want her to hide her figure behind the blacks and whites she usually wore. He could only guess that she hadn't quite come to accept her body. She hadn't said as much, but he had read between the lines. And he knew exactly how damaging that could be to a woman. To anyone.

And it was a crime—because Emma was simply stunning. So that morning, when he'd been out buying the last thing that would make this 'engagement' seem real, he'd passed a shop window and stopped in his tracks, realising at once that the dress on the mannequin was perfect.

The moment he'd seen it Antonio had wondered what Emma's curves would look like beneath the material—what the silk would reveal or conceal, what sound would it make running across her satin-smooth skin. How the colour would look against the pale cream tones of her bare arms...

The rush of his thoughts sent his body's blood south, shockingly fast, and Antonio gritted his teeth in an effort to keep himself under control and switched the shower from hot to icy cold.

And he knew—*knew* with one hundred per cent clarity—that he could not treat Emma with the same detachment that he used to handle the other women in his life. She wasn't like the women he usually took to bed. The ones who knew that he wouldn't offer them anything more.

He could no longer fool himself that it was because he was putting off anything deeper until after he had brought his father to his knees. He was self-aware enough to know that he didn't trust something as dangerous as love. It was a tool used by those more powerful, wielded to hurt, to harm.

It was as if Emma's honesty had lifted the lid on his ability to lie to himself. He knew that he had avoided anything emotional because of the power it had to be used against him. And he would never be victim to it again. But somehow Emma had managed to sneak beneath the armour he wore around his heart. To bring forth truths from his lips that he'd never shared with anyone other than Dimitri and Danyl.

And whilst everything in him wanted to run, to push her away, to save her from the darkness that threatened to consume him as he went further down his path of revenge, he knew that he wouldn't. That what he was about to do would only bind them together further.

He shut off the shower, dried himself and dressed quickly. He caught his reflection in the mirror. The perfectly tailored suit of dark blue cashmere wool matched his mood. On the bedside table was the small box that he had obtained before going to the gym.

He had thought he would simply go to the shop, make the purchase and leave. But, surprising himself, he had pored over the selection, discarding the more traditional cuts and colours and focusing instead on finding something that was unique and utterly... *Emma*. Not the PA he had spent eighteen months working with, but the woman who had hidden fire within her—the one who in fits and bursts had shown herself to be empowered... incredible, even.

He grabbed the box in his fist, then forced himself to relax his grip, hating what that said about him and his hopes for her reaction as he stalked through the suite. The tight leash on his emotions stretched taut, he called out to Emma, but didn't hear a reply.

He knocked on the door to her room, forcing himself to make it gentle and not pound on it as his heart was pounding within his chest. When there was still no answer he pushed gently on the door, ignoring the voice in his head that told him to turn back.

Smaller than his, though not by much, the room stretched out before him in rich, bold contemporary colours of black, grey and red. Emma had pushed back the curtains, revealing the night-time sky that trespassed over the race course as dusk beat a hasty retreat. Or perhaps it was Antonio who was trespassing...

He turned towards the bathroom, where he could hear the clicking of her heels on marble flooring. He was about to turn around and leave when the bathroom door opened and in walked Emma...

And his breath caught in his lungs.

She was incredible. So beautiful, so strong and powerful.

And he hated the thought that she didn't realise it.

From her feet, the deep, rich burnt orange silk bled upwards into lighter tones of amber and yellow, no less bold, but bright and eye-catching. The dress lay over her chest in a deep V, revealing the valley between her breasts. It clung to a waist that couldn't be broader than the span of his hand. It flared out from there and hung all the way to the floor.

But it wasn't until she stepped further into the room, when the high split revealed perfectly toned legs that went on for miles, that the breath that had been balled up in his chest finally escaped on an inaudible *whoosh*.

The moment she had seen the dress that had been delivered to the suite a few hours earlier her heart had almost stopped. She'd been surprised that her first reaction hadn't been instant refusal, hadn't been the thought that she could never wear such a revealing creation, but instead she was struck by how it reminded her of one of her mother's paintings. It had the same colours of the first piece her mother had produced after Emma had returned home from her last hospital stay.

There was no way that Antonio could have known about the painting, let alone the impact of the dress. But as she'd lifted the delicate material from the white box it had arrived in, and seen the way the rich golden colours shimmered in the light, she had known that she couldn't *not* wear it.

So she had put it on, and stared at herself in the mirror. Simply stared. Bold and bright, the smooth silk hugged curves she had never put on display before. For all her words the night before about being positive, about embracing the future and all it had to offer, she realised that perhaps she had left *this* behind. Allowed it to be swallowed up. That when she had thought her battle with cancer over in fact she had to continue to fight each day, to take back the things she had lost.

More than her breasts and her parents' marriage, her sensuality, her sense of self as a woman.

But now Antonio was looking at her in a way she couldn't decipher.

'How do I look?'

'Amazing,' he said without pause. 'But there's something missing.'

He reached into his trouser pocket and produced a small blue velvet box.

With trembling hands she took it from his palm, trying to avoid the zip and zing of electricity that passed between them. She laughed a little as she struggled with the little metal clasp on the box. But the moment her gaze caught the ring inside she stopped. Everything stopped.

It was a beautiful green sapphire, encased in rose gold. The precious stone was surrounded by tiny diamonds which continued the whole way around the band. It stole her breath—and in some part the walls around her heart.

'It's perfect,' she whispered as she slipped it onto her finger. She couldn't let him do it for her, it would mean too much.

'I'm pleased,' he said, holding her eyes with the same sincerity she had felt from him the night before. 'No matter what happens, I want you to keep it.'

'I…' She was speechless. 'I can't, Antonio. I don't deserve it.'

'It's not about deserve, or need. I want you to have it.'

Emma didn't know what to say. And if, somewhere deep down, there was a single tendril of sadness that this wasn't real, then that was her own fault. She'd known what she was getting into when she'd agreed to this deal. And just because she was emotional about it, it didn't change a thing.

Oh, but she wished she could.

By the time that they left the suite Emma was thankful for the reminder that their relationship was purely a business arrangement.

By the time they got to the lobby Emma had put away the childish hurt and pulled her armour back into place.

By the time the limousine arrived at the restaurant where they were to meet Bartlett, Emma was ready to do battle and slay dragons to help Antonio secure investment in Bartlett's company.

She had felt the hurt emanating from Antonio the night before as he'd told her of his childhood. She could see how important it was to him and wanted to gift him something of what he'd given her... The ability to reach for what it was that she wanted.

The lounge area of the famous Amore por la Comida restaurant spread out before them, coloured in rich amethyst hues set off perfectly by the golden twinkling stars piercing the night sky that could be seen from the windows surrounding all sides of the bar and seating areas.

The impeccably mannered head waiter was about to show them to the table when Emma felt Antonio stiffen beside her. A shiver rippled through his body like a shock wave, and she looked about them to see what might have caused it.

Coming towards them was a tall suited man she had never met before. There was something vaguely familiar about him, but she was forced to turn away from the frigid glare in his crystal blue eyes.

Instinctively she knew that this was Michael Steele, Antonio's father, and she couldn't help the way her hand slipped into the crook of Antonio's arm, as if trying to hold on to him, support him, give him something to warm the air that had suddenly cooled about them.

Antonio should have known. And perhaps deep down he had. Because his father's appearance didn't surprise him as much as it should have. He felt the drive of renewed determination fuel him. Indignation was but a second thought.

'Antonio,' Michael said as he drew close to them. 'I'd say that it's good to see you, but we both know that would be a lie.'

The charming, almost warm, smooth voice sharpened the harshness of his words.

'Why are you here?'

Antonio knew from bitter experience that the less he said to his father the better. He wondered whether Michael would have the gall to admit that he was here, at this exact place and time, because of his meeting with Bartlett. Clearly Michael had his informants, just as Antonio had his.

A cold smile graced lips that should be as familiar to Antonio as his own. In the three years since he'd last seen his father Michael Steele had grown in his mind to monstrous proportions. Instead, all he saw was an old man before him. But Antonio knew that appearances were deceiving and his whole body was on guard.

'Well, I heard rumours about the notorious Winners' Circle syndicate trying to win the hat-trick at the Hanley Cup. Surely that's a feat worth watching? If it succeeds. It would be such a shame if you were to fall at the first hurdle, so to speak. And, of course, it's a chance to catch up with old friends.'

Antonio bit back a curse. The man had absolutely no

interest in the Winners' Circle, and his allusion to 'old friends' could only mean Bartlett.

'I'm surprised you have any friends left, Michael.'

Anger had made him weak and he hadn't been able to prevent the snide comment falling from his lips.

'Come, now. There's no need to resort to childish swipes at your father.' Michael Steele barely allowed time for the reproach to strike before picking up yet another thread of venom. 'And this must be your *convenient* fiancée.'

The dismissive gesture of Michael's hands irritated him less than the fact that his father didn't even bother looking at Emma, let alone acknowledging her in any other way than by reference. Fury scoured him inside out, coursed through his veins. Antonio had long since stopped caring about the painful barbs Michael might throw in his direction, but he would not countenance any rudeness towards Emma.

'Her name is Emma. And you'll afford her the respect she deserves.'

'Respect? For a PA who miraculously becomes your fiancée when you so desperately need your reputation intact? How much did she charge you? I bet she's worth every penny of that green sapphire on her finger.'

His father's ice-cool eyes turned white-hot in a second and Antonio wanted to reach out and grab the man by the throat. But that was exactly what his father wanted. To cause a scene. To create a scandal that would make *him* look like the victim. Just the way he had done with his mother during the divorce.

Antonio had spent years studying his father's playbook, and he would not allow himself to rise to the taunt.

'Priceless,' he replied to his father's taunt.

'What?' he heard his father ask in confusion.

'Emma,' he stated, turning to her, locking his gaze with hers as if it were the only thread he could tie himself to amongst the seething emotions that were threatening to drown him.

She didn't show shock, fear or resentment—just curiosity, as if she too wanted to know what he meant.

'She is priceless. She is everything I didn't realise I needed.'

He watched as her eyes widened in surprise at his words, and hated it that he'd said them for his father—hated that he'd somehow tainted the sentiment.

'And I will not let you diminish her or hurt her. Take swipes at me, old man, or my company, but stay the hell away from her,' he growled.

For a second he saw shock in his father's eyes, but he rallied quickly.

'You think you can go up against me and win?' he snarled.

That was the voice he remembered from his childhood. The one that had haunted his sister's dreams and fuelled his own need for revenge.

'You have been nothing more than a pest, sniffing around my cast-offs. Once I win this investment with Bartlett, be assured the next business I'm coming after, *son*, is yours.'

'That's where you're wrong, *Father*. You won't win this deal with Bartlett. You've overplayed your hand and you're desperate. I can see it. And soon so will everyone else.'

Antonio unclenched his white-knuckled fist and forced himself to relax. He placed his hand on the small of Emma's back and guided her before him. He was thankful when she began to pick her way through the tables towards the head waiter, whose face betrayed no indication of hearing the conversation he must have heard.

Electricity crackled where his hand touched the almost indecently low back of her dress, but that wasn't what disturbed him. He realised that she was trembling—just slightly, not visibly—but he could feel it ripple over the soft, smooth acres of skin beneath his fingertips and he couldn't help himself.

He needed it—he needed *her*. He needed to wipe away that horrible encounter with his father. For her. For himself. He pulled her back, spinning her into him, and reached for what he so desperately wanted.

As his lips crashed down on hers he took advantage of the surprise she clearly felt, once again. How, after only one kiss, the taste and feel of her could be so familiar to him, he couldn't grasp. But his hand flew out to her cheek, holding her for his kiss, feeling her skin cool beneath the warmth of his fingers. He felt the wild flutter of her pulse beneath his palm, and satisfaction thrummed through him as it kept time with his own frantic heartbeat.

His tongue delved deeply into her mouth, relishing the way hers met and matched its every move. He didn't care that they were in a restaurant—didn't care that his father might still be watching. This wasn't for anyone else but them.

Starbursts of arousal and need crept up his spine, flaring and burning away the bitter taste of anger and resentment. And the moment her hand came up to his neck, pulling him to her as strongly as he wanted to pull her to him, he felt satisfaction, ownership, possession. A silent, primal roar sounded in his mind. *Mine*, it cried.

The realisation was startling, and enough for him to break the sensual hold that forged them together.

He drew back from their embrace, staring into eyes that were wide and dark with a desire that matched his own. Emma was breathing quickly, her cheeks flushed, and through the knowledge and the feeling of pleasure that he had done that to her, that he had caused her to feel that way, was a question ringing loudly in his mind.

Just what the hell had she done to him?

The head waiter cleared his throat discreetly and resumed his pathway towards the table where Benjamin Bartlett stood, waiting for them.

If she had known what Antonio had planned to do she would have stopped him. But, whether he'd noticed or not, the encounter with his father had unnerved her. Despite what Antonio had told her the previous night, his description of his father's cruel, ruthless behaviour, Emma had wondered if there was some reason, some explanation for his father's actions. She had thought he'd spoken with the hurt of an abandoned son, and now Emma felt terrible—as if that belief had somehow betrayed Antonio.

Because what she had seen in Michael Steele's eyes, heard in his voice, had convinced her that he was a horrible man, with no conscience nor regard for others. She understood, now, Antonio's need for revenge. Could feel it barely restrained beneath the surface of his skin. The power of it was dark, and she wished so much that he would turn away from it—even though she knew he wouldn't.

But that kiss had momentarily short-circuited her brain. Words of reassurance and support had fled beneath the sensual onslaught of his lips, and the wicked way they had demanded arousal and pleasure from her body had made her quiver with need. A need that went unsatisfied now he'd pulled away from her, leaving her wanting and shaking with desires she had never experienced before.

Realising that he had done that in public, in the middle of the restaurant full of nearly one hundred people, frustrated and angered her. But she needed to put aside that anger, because Benjamin Bartlett was there, standing at their table, waiting for them and looking decidedly uncomfortable.

And Emma was there to help Antonio win him over. Not because of the deal, and not because she was his convenient fiancée, but because she wanted to help *him*. Help him put his past to rest the way he was beginning to do for her.

She forced a smile to her lips, joy to her eyes, and took the hand Bartlett extended to her.

'Ms Guilham. It's lovely to meet you,' he said, his American accent more cultured than she had remembered from the call on the plane to Buenos Aires.

Unlike Michael Steele, Benjamin Bartlett seemed softer somehow, despite his height and lean stature. In some ways he was more like Antonio than Michael. Even though, at that precise moment in time, she could hardly say that there was anything soft about Antonio at all. In fact he seemed almost reluctant, as if still locked into an unconscious battle with his father.

'Likewise, Mr Bartlett. I hope we haven't kept you long?'

'Not at all.'

He waved them away, as if they hadn't just stood there in the middle of the restaurant kissing and instead had merely been a little delayed. And she realised then that what had made Bartlett awkward hadn't been the kiss, but the fact that he had clearly witnessed the interaction between Antonio and his father.

'I meant to ask,' Emma said as they took their seats, reaching for a conversation that she hoped would start them on potentially neutral ground, 'how is Anna's grandson? He wasn't very well the last time we spoke.'

A smile painted Bartlett's features. 'He's doing well, thank you for asking.'

Bartlett turned to Antonio, who hadn't been able to conceal his momentary confusion.

'My PA's grandson had appendicitis, and she had to stay home to care for him last week.' Turning back to Emma, he continued, 'She wanted me to pass on her congratulations. And I'd like to add mine to that,' he said, gesturing to Emma's hand.

The heavy weight of the beautiful green sapphire suddenly felt tight around her finger.

'I must admit I did wonder who it would take to make this reckless playboy settle down,' he said, but a smile took some of the sting out of his words. 'I don't believe he could have done any better.'

Emma forced some heat into her smile as guilt nibbled at her stomach. *Lying.* She was uncomfortable with lying.

'Thank you, Mr Bartlett.'

'Benjamin—please call me Benjamin,' he said, taking his seat and gesturing to them both to do the same. 'I hope you'll forgive us for talking business over our meal?'

'Of course. Antonio's very passionate about your company and I can't help but be intrigued.'

'Oh, really?' Bartlett asked.

'I have a great deal of respect for what you have

achieved,' Antonio stated, finally picking up the thread of the pitch he'd worked on non-stop for almost a week.

Phrases that Emma had heard him muttering to himself over the last few days ebbed and flowed in the conversation. They ordered drinks and food, and between the starters and the end of dessert Emma marvelled at how Antonio used his carefully constructed words to weave a spell that she was sure Benjamin Bartlett was falling under.

Each line of his pitch was carefully orchestrated, bent and moulded to the positive, outlining how Arcuri Enterprises could support, aid, help the company to grow, rather than muscle in and take over. It was skilful, almost surgical in its precision.

The warmth of Bartlett's interaction with her was very different from the careful assessment he was giving Antonio. Whilst Bartlett might be congenial, he was still a fierce businessman who was choosing his investor wisely.

'You clearly know a lot about my business, Antonio.'

'I use my research well.'

'And what does your research say about me?' Bartlett asked—and the query not one made out of vanity.

'That you are a traditional businessman who believes in keeping things the way they are. You don't like change, and you fight vehemently for your company, your brand and its continued success. You don't believe that a business deal should be done until the second bottle of whisky has been opened, and as we're in a restaurant, not a bar, and you have refused a drink with your coffee, I can tell that you haven't yet made up your mind about who is best to support you financially through the next successful stage of your business.'

Bartlett gave a surprised chuckle. 'And how did you know about the whisky?'

Antonio looked to Emma, who leaned in and said conspiratorially, 'Us PAs have our secrets, Mr Bartlett. Do allow us to keep them.'

'Ah… Of course. That is as it should be,' he replied with another warm smile.

Emma laid her fork down, defeated after less than half of the exquisite chocolate dessert she had ordered. In truth, she had neither eaten nor tasted much of the meal they had shared. Her nerves had been wound tight for Antonio. *Because* of him.

'Arcuri, it has certainly been an interesting evening. I thank you for the work you have clearly put into making this pitch, and I hope you will understand if I take this under consideration until next week. I have shareholders—many of whom see your father as a very good option.'

It was a phrase Antonio had expected, but one that was none the less unwelcome. Whether Bartlett had said it to garner a better deal from him, or whether it was the truth didn't really matter.

Yes, he'd seen desperation in his father's words and actions, but it was Dimitri's phrase that ran through his mind as he left the restaurant with Emma. That desperation made people dangerous. And he knew in that moment that he would go to any length, any extreme, to bring his father to his knees.

CHAPTER SEVEN

By THE TIME they entered the reception area of their hotel, Antonio's thoughts were no longer on Bartlett *or* his father. Something which, at one point he'd thought almost unimaginable. But that had been before they'd come to Argentina—before Emma had worn the dress he'd chosen for her, and before he'd kissed her in a crowded restaurant and wanted the whole world to burn with him.

So instead of planning his next step he was still tasting her on his tongue. Instead of feeling the black plastic key card in his fingers he was feeling her skin beneath the palm of his hand. And there was nothing he could do to relieve the ache in his chest.

Not just because Emma wasn't like the women he usually spent his nights with—women who agreed to his unemotional demands. He saw in her all the goodness, all the soft, delicate parts of her life that had come together like a silk tapestry—one that he should admire and leave untouched. She deserved someone better than him. Someone who wasn't focused on a path straight to hell…someone who wouldn't drag her there with him.

He slid the key card into the slot beside the door and walked into the suite. When he'd left earlier that night, with Emma wearing his ring, on his way to meet Bartlett, he'd imagined that when he returned he'd feel…different. That he'd feel the thrill of satisfaction at ensuring his father's destruction. That somehow meeting Bartlett would have eased the adrenaline he'd felt rushing through him for over a week—would have settled the raging beast within him.

But he didn't and it hadn't.

Instead a different kind of heat burned within him—one that made him feel just as restless and just as dangerous. He stalked over to the bar area, poured two whiskies—one over ice for Emma—and after a second thought added two ice cubes to his own, hoping to cool the fervour of his libido. In his heart, he hoped that she would refuse the drink, that she would bid him goodnight and leave him alone with his new demons.

But she didn't.

Emma closed the door behind her, turning her back momentarily on the man who had come to mean so much to her. She was buying herself time. She knew it. Had known it since before their meal with Bartlett—since the moment Antonio's lips had crashed down onto hers. Perhaps even since the previous night.

It was as if her skin was feeding off the strange tension that had been summoned by their bodies' wants and desires in the car journey back from the restaurant. The silence that had fallen between them only seemed to place a spotlight on it, illuminating what she wasn't naïve enough to dismiss.

But was she brave enough to ask—demand for herself what her body wanted?

Looking at Antonio now, standing before the large windows, his broad shoulders and lean hips accentuated by the smooth planes of his suit, staring out at the stars, she knew that it had always been going to come to this.

He had coaxed from her body things she had never imagined. He had made her feel sexy, wanted and desirable. And Emma didn't want to let go of it—didn't want to sever the strange thread that bound them together.

Her cancer had struck at a time when she had been inexperienced, and nothing and no one had tempted her since.

Until now.

And if some part of her warned that this wasn't just about claiming her body, that it was much more to do with her heart, then she ruthlessly forced that thought aside. She wanted to strike through that invisible wish on her Living List. The one that she'd never had the courage to write down, but now had the courage to ask for.

'Antonio—'

'No.'

'I haven't—'

'You don't have to say it, Emma. You *shouldn't* say it. Shouldn't ask it of me. You should go to bed.'

His tone was dark and heavy—rough like bitter coffee and as tempting as sin.

'You don't know what I'm going to ask,' she assured him…assured herself.

He turned, then. Pinned her with his hawk-like gaze. She knew it was meant to intimidate, but instead it served only to enflame.

'Really? I am a man very well versed in feminine desire, Emma. A woman does not…*you* do not need to put into words what I see in your eyes. What your body is crying out for.'

Embarrassment stung her cheeks. She had thought

that he might be as surprised as she was to find herself asking for such a thing. But he had known. Had seen it in her. Had everyone else?

But she refused to be ashamed of it. She held his gaze, used it to empower her. She felt herself stand tall against the onslaught of his presence.

'You asked me what I wanted, Antonio. Back at the gala. And yesterday you said that I had not asked anything for myself. So now I'm asking. I want *you*. This night. Just one night,' she said, leaving the rest of her thoughts unspoken.

She wanted to feel cherished…wanted to love her body. Wanted *him* to love her body.

'Do you know what you're asking, Emma?'

'Yes.'

'Do you really? A no-strings affair? Just sex? You are too innocent to know the consequences of your request.'

'I'm not going to lie and tell you that I'm experienced, because I'm not,' she said, taking a step towards his forbidding frame. 'I'm not going to lie and tell you that I'm not terrified, because I am. But I know what I want. And now I'm asking you for it. Just one night, Antonio.'

She was only asking for one night because she knew instinctively that she couldn't risk anything more. Yes, she might be inexperienced, but she knew that much.

'Emma—'

It was a plea from his lips. One that she couldn't allow herself to listen to.

She took the final step towards him, closing the distance between them. Looking up at him, standing chest to chest, she saw his lips hovering so close to her own. It was intoxicating. She'd never tasted need, actually *tasted* it on her tongue, but she knew that it would be nothing like the taste of him, his true self. Without the masks, the fakery of performance.

Her chest rose, trying to contain the beating of her heart, pushing against the silk that cleaved in a V to her breasts, as if inviting his gaze, begging for his touch. She had never felt like this. Had never felt the power of desire rushing over her skin, making her bold, making her needy.

'You said I could have anything I wanted. Please... please don't make me—' The word *beg* stuck in her throat.

She reached up, her hand cold against the hot skin of his clenched jaw. He hadn't moved a muscle, but she felt emotion swirling within him with the force of a storm. He was almost vibrating with it.

Their breathing was harsh and it echoed within the silence of the suite. Antonio's eyes were a molten mixture of fury and desire, matching her own. She allowed the heat from his body to lap against hers like a tide, threatening to overtake her and knock her down. Her mouth was inches away from his. But she wanted him to make that last move. She wanted it, needed it—needed him to prove that it wasn't just *her* in this. That he was as weak as she in this moment.

And suddenly his lips were on hers, almost punishingly. His arm snaked around her back, holding her against the onslaught of passion that was so much stronger than a tide. For a moment she basked in that power, in the feel of him encompassing her completely. She allowed it to happen to her, to shock her as his tongue demanded entrance and his body commanded surrender. Then she came to life under the sheer level of need that was binding them together.

She pushed back against the kiss, opened herself to

him. Tongue clashed against tongue, teeth nipped at lips. Her hands unclasped from his shoulders and ran down the shirt covering his chest. She pushed with one and pulled with the other, desperate to feel *more*. His hands wound their way into her hair, and she thought she might have heard a groan as he sank his hands into the sleek knot and sent the pins flying, leaving her dark auburn hair to cascade down her back.

He started to walk her backwards and she felt his strong thighs against hers in an almost erotic slide. The slit of the silk skirt parted, allowing her bare legs access to the rich material of his trousers, making her feel naked against him.

As if he, too, was thinking the same thing, one of his hands left her hair, trailed over the naked V left by the silk around her chest, down to her waist. His hand flared to span it for just a moment, before lowering even further down, skating over her hip before his fingertips traced their way to the cut in the skirt and slipped through to the bare skin of her thigh.

Emma gasped as his hand wrapped around her bottom, bringing her thigh up, allowing him to step fully between her legs, and gasped again as she felt the hard ridge of his arousal at her core. It was a promise. It was a threat.

He pulled back from their kiss, gazing down on her as if warning her that this was the point of no return, failing to realise that she'd crossed that bridge a long time back. As if her body was completely his now, her hips pressed forward against his, desperate to feel him deeper, *needing* to feel him deeper.

They came up against the arm of the sofa and he guided her back, perching her there.

'Had you asked any other man, Emma, he would

have taken you to a bed covered with roses,' he ground out against her lips, unaware that that she wouldn't have wanted that. Simply because it wouldn't have been *him*. 'Had you asked any other man, he would have showered you with gifts and seduced you with words,' he continued, unaware that he had given her the greatest of gifts, offering her words of truth instead of lies, and that it meant so much more.

'I am not that man,' he said, as if answering her thoughts. 'But,' he said, with a fierce sincerity that pinned her heart, 'I will stop at any point. Know that. You are in control here, Emma. This is your decision. If you want me to—'

She cut off his words with a kiss of her own—just as powerful, just as impassioned as any of those he had given her.

As if the last barrier had been broken, a flood of need passed between them in that kiss. His hands ran the length of her chest and breasts, down once again to the silky slit in the dress. She nearly cried out as his hands caressed the soft skin of her thighs, as his hands found the thin piece of material holding her thong together and pulled, tearing the string as if it were nothing and tossing it aside. He brought his hands down around her bottom and lifted her up against him, the material of his trousers pressed against her core, shocking her and setting a fire within her.

He stepped back, and the loss of heat from where his body had pressed against hers allowed the cool air of the room to raise goosebumps on her arms. At least that was what she told herself as she shivered against his touch. His fingers found the slick wet heat of her core, at first gently running over her clitoris, bringing an unbidden cry from her mouth.

She thought she heard him curse, but she couldn't tell. The sensations he was wringing from her body were overwhelming. She might not know what to do, but her body moved instinctively, her legs opening to his hand as his fingers mirrored his tongue as he kissed her, pushing into her, delving further and deeper. Her body arched back over his powerful arm of its own volition, pulling her away from his kiss.

Need rose deep within her, yearning, demanding something that she couldn't fathom. Her breath became gasps, and she felt unable to contain all the emotions, all the sensations within her. She cried out, his wicked sensuality bringing forth even more want, and found herself begging, pleading for something she couldn't quite name.

She barely noticed him settle between her legs, but the moment his tongue pressed against her core, wet heat against wet heat, a wildness was wrenched from her and she came apart in an explosion of white firebursts. Stars dusted the back of her eyelids and she fell into an abyss.

Antonio watched as Emma's orgasm spilled waves of shivers across her skin, flushing her cheeks with pleasure, and he was speechless. He had never seen anything so beautiful, tasted anything so sweet, experienced anything so humbling as this moment.

But as she opened her eyes, and he saw wonder and awe painted in them, he knew it wasn't enough for him to know these things. She must too.

'Do you trust me?' he asked.

'Yes,' she said simply.

He gently reached for the shoulder straps of her dress. Emma stiffened.

He knew that she was scared, embarrassed…he couldn't even begin to imagine what else she might be feeling. But he wanted to help give her back her body. He wanted her to appreciate it as it should be appreciated.

He moved slowly and gently, allowing her to get used to the idea. He pushed aside the thin straps of silk and bared her to him. He could see that she was struggling, but all he saw was perfection. Beautiful and powerful. Her breasts bore faint scars from the surgeon's knife, and as he pressed open-mouthed kisses to her skin he marvelled at the tattoos that had skilfully created nipples and areolas.

He brought his hands round to cup her breasts and nearly groaned out loud at their rightness. They felt heavy as they spilled into his hands. His thumb ran gently over her skin, and her answering shudder as it did so almost brought a smile to his lips as he bent forward and took one breast into his mouth. He laved her breasts with his tongue, first one, then the other. Emma hung her head back, pressing them further into his mouth, and he returned the favour as he pressed his groin into hers, bringing her back to him with a piercing need that nailed them both.

The sensations Emma felt were foreign and strange. She wanted his touch so much, and frustration, resentment and sadness warred in her chest. She hated it that her nipples were no longer there. This was the bit in her treasured romance books that she always skipped over. How the hero would touch, kiss and tease the heroine's nipples until they became taut and tight. She missed that feeling with an ache so deep. She hated it that her body would never be able to do that.

She had feared so much that this would hurt even more in practice than in thought. But she had been wrong. Antonio had caressed and kissed her breasts, rather than avoiding them, had touched her so much that she wasn't sure she could take it any more.

Her hands went to the silk straps of the dress. She wanted to turn away.

'Don't hide from me, Emma. You're so brave and so very strong,' he said between each kiss and caress of her breasts. 'You said that what you wanted most was this…but this isn't about me.'

She wanted to tell him that he was wrong, but in the deepest part of her she knew that he was right.

'This is about you. You've had the courage to ask for what you want…it's time to *take* what you want. It's time to stop hiding in the shadows and step into the light. You're beautiful. So beautiful, Emma…'

She hated it that his words stirred her heart, felt tears forming at the edges of her eyes, betraying her.

'I want you to say it,' he told her.

She turned her head away from him. The words were locked in a throat tight with emotion. She didn't want to say it, but Antonio asked again. Not angry, not frustrated, but with understanding and compassion shining from his eyes.

'I'm beautiful…' she whispered.

'Again, Emma,' he commanded.

'I'm beautiful,' she said, this time with a little more strength. 'I *am* beautiful,' she said, finally allowing belief to make the words strong.

Antonio scooped her up from where she was perched on the arm of the sofa and carried her through to the bedroom. And when her head rested on his chest he shook away the thought that it felt as if it had always been there.

He gently laid her on the bed, watching her eyes slowly focus on him where he stood over her, still dazed from her own empowerment and her orgasm. And even though he was so ready to take her, so ready to find his own release, he wanted her to be with him, wanted her to feel everything that he felt.

If this was his one stolen moment, then he would make it count.

Antonio's hands left her chest to pull at the edges of his shirt. Impatient to feel her skin against his, he ripped the shirt apart, sending buttons flying across the room, watching as Emma's eyes widened in both shock and arousal.

As his hands went to the waistband of his trousers, hers found the zip at the side of her dress.

'Stop,' he commanded. Her eyes found his, her cheeks painted red with desire and perhaps just a trace of embarrassment. He leaned forward. 'That's for me to do, Emma. That's *my* pleasure.'

He leaned back and brought down the zip on his trousers, relishing every second as she watched him slowly push them off his legs. He watched her restless legs, sliding up and down against each other as if the friction might get close to the pleasure he could administer.

He smiled knowingly, stepping forward, pressing her thighs apart and bringing the palm of his hand to rest at her centre.

Emma jerked her hips against the contact of his hot palm between her legs. There was nothing but the autumnal silk of the dress between his skin and hers, slick and ready.

He sat on the bed next to her, reaching around to her side and slowly, ever so slowly, releasing the dress's zip from its casing, drawing it down to where it ended at the top of her hip. His hands swept under the material, feeling their way across her stomach and up to her breasts. He moved one hand down in between her legs and parted her there with his fingers.

As her hips rose off the bed to meet his hand he swept the burnt orange silk from beneath her, moved it up above her waist with his other hand. He brought her breast to his mouth and whipped the material over her head as he savoured her breasts, relishing each cry that fell from Emma's lips.

He gathered the dress in his fist and threw the crumpled silk onto the floor, then leaned back and took her small dainty feet in his hands. He stroked the insides of her feet and placed them apart, moving in between her legs. As his hands caressed their way up her calves, over her knees and up her thighs, Emma sighed, watching his hands work their way up over her hips towards her breasts, her spine arching off the bed, pressing them into his palms.

For what seemed like hours he stayed there, caressing, licking, tasting all that she had to offer. Watching her both lose herself and find herself in the passion they were creating together.

Reluctant to leave the soft satin of her skin, he leaned towards the bedside table and took protection, tearing off the foil and positioning the latex over himself. Her small hands came over his as he rolled the condom over his length, her fingers wrapping around his erection, smoothing down to the base.

Before she could chip any more away from the last

shreds of his will power he picked up one of her hands, whilst positioning himself at her slick core.

He looked at her, silently begging her... For refusal or acceptance, he didn't know any more. Her hands slid around him, clasping his hips and gently pulling him towards her, sealing their fate.

As he slowly pushed himself between her thighs he kissed the inside of her palm and entered her so carefully it was almost torture. But it wasn't torture at all. It was bliss. She was so wet, so ready for him, and he sank deep into the tight, wet heat of her, allowing her body to shift and make room for him entirely.

Never before had he felt so deeply connected, so deeply *with* someone. And something inside him shifted. Something he couldn't allow to take hold.

He inched forward just a little more, and Emma's eyes widened and locked on to his.

He waited for her to acclimatise to him, and when he saw that she had he withdrew and plunged back into her, deep and hard. Her cries of pleasure rang out in the room, urging him on, into her again and again. An incredible sensation was stretching throughout his body, taking a firm hold on his chest and what lay hidden there beneath his ribs, and he knew—*knew* that this wasn't just sex.

His cries soon joined hers and he grasped her wrists, holding them above her head, staring down into her eyes. He couldn't hold back any more—he couldn't hold *anything* back any more.

Sensing that she was on the brink of her second orgasm, feeling the tightening of her muscles around him, hearing that special, perfect pitch of her voice, he thrust into her one last time, and they fell together even more deeply over the edge than ever before.

* * *

Antonio woke in a panic. His heart pounded in his chest, a cold sweat gathered on his brow, and his head was filled with thoughts of his father cruelly ripping him from Emma's sleep-fuelled embrace.

It took him a moment to place himself. A thing that had never happened to Antonio before in his life. Not when he, his mother and sister had been wrenched from America and sent back to Italy...not in any of the numerous hotel rooms where he had spent countless nights for his business.

But the fear didn't recede. Unaccountably, Antonio couldn't shake the feeling that something awful was on the horizon—waiting to crash down and blow everything to smithereens.

Emma turned beside him, the smooth sleek line of her spine exposed where he had pulled the sheets back from their stranglehold around his chest. He needed to move, needed to leave the safe haven of her bed, was reluctant to somehow infect her with his thoughts.

He grabbed his trousers from where he'd thrown them off only hours before and padded his way through to the living room, gently closing the door on the passion and emotion of earlier hours.

He forced his legs into the trousers and fastened the zip and the button around his waist. Signs of their lovemaking were everywhere. Discarded clothes, rumpled paper and documents from the Bartlett deal neither of them had seen in the urgency of their need.

He paced the room. Back and forth. And still couldn't shake the feeling of impending doom. His father had something. Something that Antonio didn't. Something on Bartlett, he decided. He was too self-assured for a man on the brink of destruction. That was what had bothered him most about his father. Yes, he'd seen desperation—but he'd also seen triumph.

And then he did something he'd never thought himself capable of.

He found his mobile phone amongst the chaos of the room and pulled up the number of Arcuri Enterprises' private investigator.

Not caring what time it would be in America, he spoke quietly and efficiently, outlining his need for the man to dig up anything and everything he might be able to find on Bartlett, or his family. Only days ago Emma had pointed out that Bartlett's daughter was something of a party girl. She might be on to something.

If Antonio felt any guilt then he forced such a feeling aside, bringing to mind instead that horrible confrontation with his father. The only way to fight a monster was to become one himself. His father would pay for what he'd done. And if that meant reducing himself to his father's level, ruining his soul, Antonio was willing to do so.

CHAPTER EIGHT

CLASH OF THE TYCOON TITANS!
BY *ROANNA KING*

Arcuri vs Steele, son against father,
who will win?

It would seem that Antonio Arcuri's shock engagement was just the beginning. The business world is holding its breath as father and son pitch for the same deal! Sources close to the tycoons have suggested a last-ditch battle of wills.

For years Arcuri has nipped at the edges of Steele's business dealings, and is now pulling out all the stops to slash and burn with his legendary ruthlessness—his father, no less.

And while women around the world are still mourning the loss of this international bachelor, men are salivating, placing bets on who will draw first—and last—blood.

With so much on the line for these two men, it will certainly be a clash of the tycoon titans!

DIMITRI'S GREEK-ACCENTED VOICE rose above the hum of the crowds as he read the article out loud, clearly just for the hell of it.

'At least they didn't mention Bartlett by name,' he noted.

'I doubt very much that it was by mistake or from some inherent sense of propriety. This has the stink of my father all over it,' Antonio growled.

'He must be desperate if he's willing to risk such exposure, given how notoriously private Bartlett is,' Danyl reflected, looking out at the race course from the balcony of the hospitality suite set aside for the Winners' Circle.

Discreet servers had placed trays of delicate food there, none of which was appealing to Antonio at that moment. He shifted his sunglasses back over his eyes.

Danyl turned in his seat beside him, pinning him with a powerful gaze. 'You have something to hide?'

'No,' came Antonio's terse reply.

Danyl gave a spectacularly *un*-regal grunt in response, and placed a Bloody Mary on the table in front of him. 'Hair of the horse that bit you, so to speak.'

Antonio ignored them both and took a mouthful of the thick, spicy tomato juice.

'Virgin?' queried Dimitri as Danyl rolled his eyes.

The sting of tabasco sauce caught Antonio in the back of the throat and he forced himself to swallow the drink through a throat thick with convulsions.

'For God's sake, Dimitri.'

The sounds of the crowd and the announcements over the Tannoy drifted up from the race course below.

'Did anyone see Mason this morning?' Antonio asked, when in truth his mind had been searching for Emma. Emma whom he'd left sleeping in the hotel room while he'd sneaked out like a thief.

'John was guarding her like a dog. He wouldn't let anyone near her this morning. Said something about not letting us "psych her out".'

'Us or you, Danyl?' Dimitri asked. 'You still haven't said how you know her.'

'I still haven't said that I *do* know her.'

Antonio let the sounds of his friend's light-hearted squabble fall over him as he tried to block out the memory of Emma's sighs of pleasure that still, even now, thickened his blood.

He clenched a fist, trying to regain control of his errant body. He couldn't believe what madness had overtaken them last night. He'd promised her only one night, but now he wondered if he could keep that promise. It wouldn't last—it couldn't. He would only end up hurting her, letting her down, drawing her deeper into his own need for revenge.

'You might want to put that glass down, Antonio,' Dimitri said, his words cutting through the emotional fog that was surrounding him.

'Mmm?'

'The glass. If you carry on, it might just crack.'

Antonio looked down to see white knuckles encasing thin glass and put the drink back on the table. Danyl was looking at him with a raised eyebrow, wry curiosity painting his features.

'Dare I ask how the Bartlett deal is going?'

'Actually, our meeting went very well. Even after my father made his surprise guest appearance.'

Concerned silence met his statement. Danyl and Dimitri were watching and waiting for the explanation they knew he would give them. They alone knew the depths of his hatred for his father, the true extent of which he hadn't been able to confess to Emma.

They greeted his account with an anger and fury that matched his own. And Michael Steele's treatment of Emma was high on their list of his crimes.

'Are you sure you want to go that way?' Dimitri asked when Antonio confessed the action he had directed his PI to.

'If there's anything to find you can be sure that Michael will have already discovered it, and he will plan to use it to his advantage.'

'And are you willing to do the same? To use blackmail to get what it is that you want?'

A commotion at the paddock drew their attention and prevented Antonio from needing to answer Dimitri's question. As Antonio recognised Mason's colours and Veranchetti's proud stance he forced all other thoughts from his mind.

Emma wove her way through the throng of people in the stands towards the stairs to the hospitality suite, where she knew Antonio and his friends—the Winners' Circle syndicate—would be. The day was beautiful, despite the bad weather forecasted for later. It was strange to think that there could be anything like rain on the horizon when the air, despite being stirred up by the spectators, was calm and the sun was strong.

She felt a laugh rise within her chest and stifled it. Here she was, in a sea of people, and no one was looking at her because of what she lacked. She was invisible. And yet she felt as if she knew a secret that no one else did.

Throughout the night she had reached for Antonio, had felt him reach for her, and they had teased and taunted each other to completion more times than she could believe. Those precious hours were a montage of sensation and feeling, always with the heat of Antonio beside her, over her, behind her. It was as if her body had craved that warmth, needed it to come alive again.

She felt re-made—re-worked in a way she couldn't have expected. It was as if an old ache around her heart had lessened and she felt lighter than she had done in years.

She had woken alone and hadn't been surprised, realising that on some level she must have heard him leave. A web of nerves had tightened around her stomach. How would they be the next time they encountered each other?

No, she thought now, pressing a hand against her belly to quell the butterflies. She wouldn't be embarrassed about last night. They were adults. And what they had shared was incredible. Antonio had made her see herself in a way she had never done before and that was something more precious than she ever could have realised.

She felt strong and, yes, even a little giddy. Last night she had seen him, Antonio Arcuri, as needy and as aroused as her. She had met him as an equal and nothing would take that away. And to be his equal—not his PA, and not his fake fiancée? It thrilled her.

Was this what love was? *Desire*, she hastily corrected herself. A high that made her feel powerful, strong? She relished that feeling and all of a sudden her chest was fit to burst. Excitement swept through her as she began to climb the steps towards the balconies bordering the race course.

Her heart pulsed within her chest and she wondered how anyone could live like this, in this constant state of awareness and excitement. Would it go away? Would it dim over time? Did she want it to?

For so long, so many years, she had wanted to feel this way. Wanted to own herself, to feel cherished and desired. Somehow, despite her optimism and determination to experience all that life had to offer, she had let herself hide from the one thing that she had truly wanted.

Here she was, on the brink of having it all, and suddenly she felt the fear that it could all be taken away. And that was when she knew just how much she had sacrificed—just how much she had pushed deep down within her, ignoring the wants and desires that she craved.

This man—hell-bent on revenge, but capable of the tenderness of last night—had stolen her heart. The goodness in him that she could see made those feelings even more powerful. She wanted him to win the Bartlett deal against his father. Not because of the hatred that Antonio felt for him, but to put an end to it so that Antonio could move on.

Even from this high up Antonio could imagine—could remember—the feeling of sitting on top of a powerful horse pawing at the ground with shod hoofs, the flex of the animal's muscles beneath the saddle, the creaking of leather, the way a horse would lift and shift beneath him. The thrilling rush of adrenaline that would pound through both him and the horse together, as one. That moment just before the horse would pull back, ready to launch itself forward, ready to catapult into a gallop and leave just about everything behind.

At one point in his life riding had meant freedom—escape from a father who had made his and his mother's and sister's lives a misery. In the end, he realised, he'd not escaped anything.

As the noise picked up around the grounds, mixing with incoherent announcements from the Tannoy, Antonio battled with the past and the present. Somehow he knew that it was all rooted in the events of the night

before. Bartlett, his father, Emma, business, passion…
All of it was making him feel as if he were on some
precipice, and he couldn't tell whether he was about to
be saved or doomed.

The shrill of the bell signalling the start of the race
cut through the stands as the barriers on the starting
gate opened and the horses leapt forward.

For just a moment the breath caught in his lungs.

But it wasn't because of the race.

He felt her presence behind him, as she stepped out
on to the balcony that jutted out over the course below.
He teased himself, holding himself back from the moment when he would turn and look at Emma. A test of
sorts. One that he failed.

She was dressed in a white sleeveless top with dark
blue flowing trousers. Her thick dark hair swirled
around her. She raised her hand to catch at the strands,
sweeping them back from her face as she looked down
at the horses, rather than at him.

His heart thumped painfully in his chest as tension
ran through the crowd on a ripple that reached all the
way to the balcony. Urgency filled the air, and the noise
created by the people reached higher towards a cre-
scendo that, just for a moment, he thought might never
find its peak.

And still he could not take his eyes from the woman
who had come to stand beside him. He felt her on his
skin, through the layers of his clothes, over the hours
since they had shared a bed. The bed he wanted to take
her back to and never leave.

Suddenly her body sprang into action. Both arms
were raised and she was punching into the air, her cry
of surprise matched only by the furious yells of the two
men beside him. A fist thumped on his back—Dimitri,

lost in his excitement. And Danyl was staring deep into
the winner's gate, as if not really sure he had seen Mason
McAulty lead Veranchetti to victory.

Antonio hadn't. All he'd seen was Emma. And he
shuddered as a cold bead of sweat trickled down his spine.

He watched with an unwarranted anger unfurling in
his stomach, seeing Danyl and Dimitri sweep Emma
up into swift, joyous embraces. The small balcony suddenly seemed overly full as waiters descended with bottles of champagne and hands reached over the balcony
walls to offer congratulations and cheers of success.

A possessive streak he hadn't realised he owned
coursed through his body. If he'd noticed the flash of
the cameras, he couldn't say. If he'd told himself it was
for appearances' sake, rather than the desperate need
to feel her lips against his, it would have been a lie.

He pulled her to him—a move that was becoming
increasingly familiar and ever more welcome—until
he was an inch…a breath…away from a kiss that he
already knew would enflame the burning furnaces of
his desire. Something that would have the power to take
away the painfully fierce anger boiling in his chest as he
thought of his father, as he thought of his own actions.

He teased them both, watching the hazel flecks of
her eyes dissolve into sea-green depths. Over the din,
the shouts and cries of the crowd around them, he heard
her gasp, saw the moment surprise sizzled into expectation and want, and pushed the moment further. To
when nothing else could be seen, heard or felt—when
it was just the two of them.

When he could make her realise that this wasn't for
the press, for Bartlett, for anyone else other than him
and her.

And then he took what he so desperately wanted.

* * *

Emma felt her hand creep up towards Antonio's neck, pulling him deeper, forging them together with tongue and teeth. She laved his tongue with her own, brought the thumb of her other hand to the corner of his mouth, relishing the sensual power she wielded now, daring him to taste her. Taste more of her.

She gave no thought to anyone around them, no feeling for the concern as to where this might lead, and it thrilled as much as terrified her. She matched his almost desperate movements with her own, taking everything he had to give and offering her all in return.

He had turned her into a wanton woman and she shamelessly claimed him for the world to see. She wanted to imprint herself on him, wanted to eradicate the memory of all who had come before her. Wanted to be the only thing he needed.

'That's enough, you two,' Dimitri called out, bringing Emma crashing back to the present.

She slowly pulled back, satisfaction stretching through her to see Antonio Arcuri as dazed and shocked as she felt.

'No,' she whispered, for his ears only. 'It's not enough,' she said with a gentle shake of her head—before she turned a beaming smile on Antonio's friend and relinquished her hold on Antonio to accept a glass of champagne .

'Gentlemen. Congratulations,' she said, in a surprisingly steady voice.

Three hours later and the promised storm had bruised the sky a deep purple, but for all its bluster it had still failed to break. The wind was whipping up the leaves around the trees that lined the streets below, reminding

Antonio of the crowds of people surrounding the winner's gate earlier. The press had burst upon them in a hail of flashbulbs, firing questions about the next two races, to be carefully deflected by three men who knew better than to engage with the paparazzi.

Mason McAulty, the female jockey whose name was now on everyone's lips, had been discreetly spirited away by John, moved on to prepare for the next race in Ireland almost before her feet had left Veranchctti's stirrups.

Danyl, who had watched her go with the same frantic energy of the storm, had barely commented on the win—as if both relieved and concerned by it—and had simply stalked through the halls of The Excelsus towards the private function room that had been prepared for the closing event of the Hanley Cup's first leg.

It was a glamorous affair, attended by royal dignitaries, international syndicates, horse breeders and owners. Models hung from arms like accessories, but none took Antonio's notice. A waiter passed by with a tray full of the finest champagne, but even the promise of cool nutty flavours and frothy light bubbles wasn't enough to disguise the taste of Emma still on Antonio's tongue.

It was addictive. He wanted more. And he *never* wanted more.

He made his way over to the bar, looking for a drink that would succeed in refocusing his tastebuds. Bartlett would be there to celebrate the Winners' Circle's success, although he was still to confirm whether he would choose his father or him. But Antonio knew. He would be chosen in the end. He was now sure of it.

Dimitri was at the bar, his brooding presence enough to create a wide berth around him, clear of people. Danyl was still looking out over the race course through the windows as the first drops of promised rain slung themselves against the glass. In contrast to the gloss and sheen of revelry that dusted the other guests, the members of the Winners' Circle seemed consumed by their own demons.

Dimitri reached behind the bar, ignoring the frown from the barman busy with another customer, grabbed a glass and poured Antonio a drink from the bottle of obscenely expensive whisky beside him. Dimitri threw an impressive stack of pesos onto the bar, which mollified the barman.

'Why does this feel like a wake rather than a victory?' Dimitri demanded. 'Come on—we're celebrating!'

Antonio cast a glance in Dimitri's direction. There was a light in his eyes that Antonio hadn't seen for far too long. 'What is it?'

Dimitri's gaze was fierce. 'They got him! The SEC have finally brought civil charges against Manos,' he said, spitting out the name of his half-brother, 'and my name is finally and completely cleared.'

'Now, *that* I can drink to,' Danyl said, and he leaned over and poured himself a large helping of whisky.

'It's been a long time coming,' Antonio added, 'but well worth the wait.' He savoured the burn of the alcohol in his throat.

'I'm sorry that I can't stay for longer,' said Danyl. 'I have to fly home. My mother has been talking about brides and babies again.'

Dimitri choked on his drink. 'Nothing, and I mean *nothing*, would tempt me into taking a bride, let alone having a baby,' he said, slamming his glass down on the bar. 'But it seems that the same cannot be said for Antonio.'

He felt the weight of both men's gazes on him. 'It's

just for show. Bartlett needed reassurance to get him to the table—Emma offered that.'

He saw Dimitri's eyes lock onto something over his shoulder. 'I don't think that's the only kind of enticement she's offering,' Dimitri replied.

Antonio's stomach clenched even before he had seen her—awaiting, expecting, the punch to the gut he had begun to experience each time he caught sight of her. The hair on his neck prickled as he forced himself not to immediately turn towards the entrance to the bar. Holding off the moment for as long as possible…both punishment and penance.

'You bloody fool,' Danyl said.

'What?' Antonio asked.

'You've slept with her,' Dimitri accused.

Finally lifting the leash on his body, Antonio turned to watch her enter the room. She was wearing the midnight-blue lace dress he'd seen her try on in the dressing room the other day. It wrapped around her skin as if it had been painted on, and yet there was nothing indecent about it. Only the reaction it had caused in him.

Because although he was an experienced man, and he'd had his fair share of women, nothing he'd seen until that moment had made him want to back a woman into the nearest room, throw out any people in the near vicinity and rip the clothing from her body.

And Antonio had the unnerving suspicion that she knew it too. She was taunting him in that dress, making him want to take back his promise from only hours before…the promise that they could only ever have one night. Because right then he wanted to live that night over and over and over again.

He watched her walk over to Bartlett, rather than avoiding the man as he himself had done so far. He

nearly flinched when she laid her hand on his arm, offering him a smile that was both familiar and pleased.
When she whispered something in his ear, eliciting a
fond reaction from Bartlett, Antonio nearly broke a wis-
dom tooth because his jaw was clenched so hard.

'She's making some powerful friends, Arcuri,' Dimitri warned. 'You'd better watch out.'

Antonio couldn't take his eyes off her as she turned
in their direction and wove through the tables dotted between them. And she held his gaze for all she was worth,
right until she stopped barely a foot away from him.
Then she turned her amazing smile on his companions.

'Gentlemen,' Emma said by way of introduction, 'how
far into the celebrations are we? Starting gate or halfway?'

'A little bit of both. Emma, I must say, you look rav-
ishing!'

'Why, thank you, Dimitri. As always, you look devastatingly handsome.'

'Careful—if you carry on being so charming I might
have to steal you away from Antonio myself.'

She laughed, and laughed even more when she heard
Antonio's answering growl. If she'd ever wondered what
it might feel like to be the centre of his world... Well...
She was beginning to feel it now.

'What's your poison, Emma?' Dimitri asked, and
for all the outward brooding she had seen in him from
across the bar when she'd first entered, there was something almost kind in his eyes.

She took in their glasses, and the outrageously expensive bottle of whisky, but decided against the heady
amber liquid she now associated with dark nights and
deep secrets.

'Prosecco, please.'

The barman nodded, and placed a full flute on the bar.

She turned to Danyl. 'Your Highness,' she said, with a small bow of her head, knowing from experience that anything more overt would rankle. For someone who held such a public position, the Sheikh of Terhren was a deeply private man.

'My assistant wishes to pass on his congratulations and his immense relief,' said Danyl. 'He is very much looking forward to a time when he no longer has to do battle with you. You have knocked his considerable confidence in his own abilities.'

She knew it was flattery, gentle and teasing, and it felt so good to be amongst Antonio's friends. It wasn't often that she saw this side of her fiancé—her *boss*—she hastily corrected herself. Though she couldn't really say that he was her boss any more. Last night had put an end to that and replaced stern reminders of her place with delicate strands of hope. Hope that this could be so much more.

She turned to greet Antonio and the words stuck in her throat. He looked so sexy, so powerful. He hadn't changed, as she had, and was still dressed in the same dark trousers and shirt open at the collar that he had been wearing earlier that day. But where before there had only been traces of stubble, now a dark shadow covered the planes of his cheeks and strong jawline and her fingers itched to reach out, to touch the deliciously rough edges.

She didn't have to wonder what he thought of the dress. It was all there in his eyes. It was the same struggle she'd had when she'd looked in the mirror before coming to the bar. Was this the right thing to do? Was she brave enough to take what she wanted and damn the consequences?

Looking at Antonio in that moment, she felt a smile pull at the edge of her lips. One that found a quick answer.

He leaned in and bent his mouth to her ear. The warmth of his breath threw cold shivers down her back as his words reached her.

'You're going to pay for wearing this dress later,' he warned darkly.

'Is that a promise?' she enquired innocently, while the devil in her danced.

'Oh, so much more than a promise, Emma,' he said, before returning to the circle of his friends.

Something like relief spread through her chest. It was all going to be okay. Dimitri pressed her glass into her hand and drew back to make room for her at the bar. No, she decided, it was going to be more than okay.

Antonio watched Emma chat happily with two of the world's most powerful men and wondered how she could ever have doubted herself. The promise he'd made to her, warning her that it would only ever be one night, was turning to ash, leaving only the taste of anticipation on his tongue. He wanted her. He would have her. Tonight.

And suddenly it seemed that it was all possible. That he'd get the Bartlett deal, that he would wreak his revenge on his father, that he might even get to keep Emma for a while. He could certainly make her happy—perhaps help her tick off some more of the things on her Living List.

Pleasure uncoiled in his chest—a different kind from what he was used to. This wasn't the thrill of the chase, or the knowledge that he had won some kind of challenge. It was the kind of pleasure he'd experienced only a few times as a child at being given something… Something precious…a gift without strings. And he wanted to unwrap that present. Right now.

Some hours later Emma was making her way back to the bar from the bathroom when the concierge found her.

'Ms Guilham, there is a package for Mr Arcuri at reception. We didn't want to interrupt him.'

Emma looked in Antonio's direction, and seeing him surrounded by his friends, laughing with a lightness she hadn't seen from him for quite some time, she understood the concierge's quandary.

'Are you happy for me to sign for it?' she asked, and when he agreed she followed him out of the bar and through the much quieter halls to Reception.

The sudden silence of the corridor made her feelings of happiness seem so much bigger, so much harder to contain. She had enjoyed talking to his friends, the feeling of being amongst them. The bond they shared was so clear and so strong it was a wonder to her. And she questioned for the first time whether perhaps it was *she* who had caused the distance between her and her friends from school, that perhaps *she* had kept that distance.

Emma decided that enough was enough. No more hiding when there was so much joy, so much of this indescribable feeling to experience.

The concierge reached behind the desk and produced a thin manila envelope, along with an electronic pad for her to sign on receipt.

She gently pulled the envelope open and, seeing the name 'Bartlett' on the cover sheet of the papers in neat handwritten capitals, didn't think anything of it. Not for a moment did she consider that it was something she shouldn't see.

But as she pulled out the documents inside the folder she realised just how wrong she had been.

CHAPTER NINE

ANTONIO HAD STARTED to wonder where Emma had got to about an hour ago. Danyl had left—he was returning to Terhren—and Dimitri had turned his attentions to a rather beautiful Iranian woman.

Antonio had no intention of blocking his pursuit. Ever since Dimitri's imprisonment a cloud had hung about him. And the news of his half-brother's involvement in his imprisonment had not done as much as he'd thought to lighten it.

Unease started to nibble at the edges of the excitement he'd felt earlier in the evening. It wasn't like Emma simply to disappear. He knew he hadn't missed her amongst the glittering, bejewelled guests at the Hanley Cup's closing party. He had lost that sense of her. That he could feel her presence should have been warning enough. But the fact that he couldn't...

He made his way back to the suite, his heart pounding, aware that something must be terribly wrong. Which was perhaps why he was not surprised to find the rooms shrouded in darkness when he entered.

Emma stood in front of the huge windows, illuminated by the bursts of lightning that fired through the night sky. The storm that had been promised was finally breaking.

His gaze caught a glimpse of the private investigator's dossier on the side table—open. And that was the moment he knew that everything he thought he might have had, everything that had made him feel so much hope, was about to slip through his fingers. Not just the Bartlett deal, but Emma too.

In the time it took for another burst of lightning to burn through the night-time sky he realised suddenly just how much she had come to mean to him—how much he wanted her to be his. And not just until after the deal…after Hong Kong. He wanted to show her the world. He wanted to help her achieve everything on her Living List. He wanted to make her his for ever.

But then he saw her bags, packed and waiting by the door to her room, and knew he'd been foolish to allow himself to think such thoughts. He could never have her—not whilst seeking his father's punishment. He could never have her and still do the things that needed to be done—to become a monster to catch a monster. But it didn't stop him from wanting to try.

'What is this?'

Her voice cut through the silence. The question echoed in the burst of thunder that rolled across the race course outside.

'Emma—'

'What *is* it?' she demanded, her voice suddenly more powerful and commanding than the elements raging beyond the windows.

'It's a file I requested to be compiled on Bartlett.'

'Do you not think that you offered the best deal to Bartlett?' she asked.

'Yes.'

'Do you not think that you deserve to win this contract on your own merit?'

'Yes,' he growled, his anger, his fear, all working to meet her tone.

'Then explain to me what *that* is.'

'It's insurance.'

'Insurance?' she spat.

He had never heard her tone so dark, so angry, and he hated that he had made it so. Hated that he had tainted her in any way because of his need for revenge.

'That isn't insurance. That is the complete and abject desecration of a person, Antonio. Your PI has dug up dirt on Mandy Bartlett and—what? You were going to use it to blackmail Bartlett into letting you invest in his company?'

He met her accusations with silence. There were no shields to protect him from the truth of her words.

'Is this because of what I said the other night? Because I followed her on social media and saw that she was young and foolish?'

The heartbreak in Emma's voice was too much for him to bear. But he simply couldn't tell her that she was wrong.

'Did it give you a lead to where your PI should look?'

'Yes,' he said, the word drawn from the very depths of his soul.

She turned her back to him and finally he glanced at the open folder—pictures of a young student spilled from it. Snapshots of a small blonde partying with her friends. And while one or two showed a happy, fun-loving girl, a few he could see peeking out beneath showed that she had started to experiment with drugs, that images of her scantily clad, showed her in poses that were highly salacious.

The thought of sharing them with the girl's father turned his stomach.

But the accusation, the pressure of the weight in Emma's eyes made him angry. Angry that his father had forced him to this—angry at himself. So he turned that anger and used it against Emma.

'It's hypocrisy. That *I* needed *you* to make me seem more palatable to Bartlett when his daughter is—'

'Stop,' Emma commanded, her hand coming up between them to accentuate her words unconsciously. 'Stop right there. It's *not* hypocritical to hold to a moralistic lifestyle while another human being chooses not to. This is a young girl taking a bad path. Those frozen snapshots aren't the whole picture of who she is and what she will be. Though they will be the *only* picture if you give them to her father.'

She was almost out of breath. She desperately wanted him to see what he was doing, to see where he was going. It was a path she wasn't sure he was going to come back from.

'Mandy Bartlett is a young girl making mistakes and hopefully she will learn from them. What she is *not*, Antonio, is a pawn to be used in a sick game between you and your father.'

'It is not a sick game, Emma. My father deserves to burn in hell for what he did.'

'Because he left you? Antonio, I realise that it must have—'

'No!' he roared. 'This isn't about him leaving, nor blackening my mother's name, nor forcing us to leave our home. *Dio*, we could have handled that. But Cici… She had more than just nightmares after the divorce,' he said, his voice hoarse with the emotion he had bottled up for years.

* * *

As if it were yesterday he remembered his mother's frantic phone call from Italy, just six months into his time in New York, begging him to come home immediately. She had been incoherent, and the only thing he'd managed to gather was that Cici was in hospital.

Nothing—*nothing*—had ever made him feel so terrified as those seven hours on the private jet Danyl had secured for him.

Until he'd seen the sight of his sister's small, impossibly emaciated frame. The doctors had explained that she must have been hiding it for years.

Antonio had known *exactly* how long she'd been hiding her eating disorder from them. At sixteen she'd weighed less than she had at thirteen, when Michael had changed their lives for ever.

And he'd not known. He'd not seen it.

His mother had been as truly shocked as he, and together they'd spent the next two weeks not leaving her side. The sounds of his sister's sobs had cut him deeply. He just hadn't been able to comprehend the negative sense of self coming from his once fun-loving, happy sister.

She had taken all the hurt and all the pain of her father's rejection, of being cut off from her friends and the life she had once known, and turned it in on herself. And he'd felt…angry and furious. He had known exactly who was to blame and had vowed to have his revenge.

Antonio hadn't realised that he'd been speaking—saying the words of his mind out loud to Emma in the suite—until he felt the rawness in his throat, saw the gathering tears framing her eyes.

She crossed the distance between them in quick

strides and wrapped her arms around him. Her body gave warmth and life to his that had turned so cold. She pressed kisses to his neck, pulling his mouth to hers, and he greedily consumed what she had to offer.

This kiss was so different from those that had passed between them before. Not one borne of a selfish need for satisfaction, of the infernal heat of their desires, but one of warmth, of comfort, of support and the one thing he could not bring himself to name.

He sought out the areas of her skin not concealed by the lace fabric of the dress. He needed to feel her beneath him, to take every comfort she was offering and more. In their kiss he tasted the salty sweetness of her tears, evidence of her grief for him and perhaps even of his own.

'I'm sorry,' she whispered against his lips. 'So sorry that you and Cici had to go through that.'

And he felt it down in the darkest part of his heart— her words beginning to shine a soft light on a place he'd thought unreachable. The place he'd thought irrevocably damaged by his father, by shock and fear for his sister.

Emma's heart had wrenched open at the sight of Antonio in such pain. He was on a precipice—one foot on land and one hovering above an abyss. Her only thought at that very moment was to comfort, to love the man she knew he could be—the man torn apart by a sense of injustice, the man who was devastated by the consequences of the careless actions of his father.

Her hands traced the lines of his strong jaw. His skin was cold to her touch, as if his memories had leached the warmth from his body. She imbued her kisses with every emotion she felt for him, desperate to show him that love had the power to heal. Not with words. Antonio wasn't ready for words. But with actions, deeds.

For just a moment he seemed simply unable to accept what she had to offer, and she wondered if she might not be able to reach him. Then, on a deep shudder, as if a barrier had fallen down and crumbled through his body, she felt his hands on her body. Touching, caressing, pulling her towards him.

Soft warmth turned to molten heat and threatened to consume them both whole.

Pulling him gently within her embrace, she walked them backwards towards her room, sidestepping the bags she'd placed there only an hour before. She drew him further, feeding him with need and desire and the love she felt for him.

Her hand went to her hair, releasing the pins that held it in place, allowing it to tumble down around her shoulders and arms. She found the discreet zip hidden at her side and pulled it down, peeling the lacy fabric from her skin.

His gaze seared her as she stood before him but she bore it, stood tall and proud beneath it. Wearing only panties and her heels, she felt no sense of the self-consciousness she had experienced the first time they had come together. There wasn't even a thought to her breasts or her femininity. There was only her need for him, her love for him, and it felt more powerful than anything she had experienced before. She revelled in the way his gaze ravaged her body—not just one part, not just *that* part, but all of her. As if he were seeing her for the very first time.

But he seemed struck still by the storm of emotion she read in his eyes. Not unsure, but unmoving. So she crossed to him, her hands going to the buttons of his shirt, undoing them so that she could feel the warmth and heat of his powerful chest. She marvelled at the light but rough dusting of hair beneath her fingers, at the way his heart raged beneath her hand. She followed the hollowed dips to the waistband of his trousers and unbuckled their fastening.

Throughout all of it he had yet to move, as if he were simply incapable of it. But tension and energy pulsed beneath his skin, begging for release, demanding it.

She left the trousers open and returned to his chest, pushing the shirt from his body, relishing the way he shivered beneath her touch, warmed beneath her kisses. But still he held himself back from her in a vice-like grip of control.

He was so glorious. Standing shirtless in her room. Her fingers traced the span of his upper arms, the defined muscles of his torso, the tense muscle offering such power and protection. She wanted to feel his arms about her, wanted to be in his embrace.

And suddenly, as if he'd heard her need, her desire, Antonio swept his arms around her, holding her to him as his open-mouthed kisses plunged the hollows of her neck. Electric currents matched only by the lightning crashing outside the windows licked up her spine and across her exposed skin.

In the space of a heartbeat he had taken control—or lost it. Emma couldn't really be sure. He devoured her with his touch, fed on her as a starving man would his first meal. He walked her back to the bed and came down on it with her, not once breaking the contact of his lips.

His hands and mouth worshipped her body, exploring every inch of her. She kicked off her shoes, leaving only the small thong covering her modesty. His hands gently pressed her thighs apart and he pressed hot wet

kisses against the material. Her own answering wet-
ness was no longer an embarrassment, simply a declaration of her desires and needs. He teased her through
the fabric, making her desperate to remove this last
barrier between them.

She groaned—or he did. Their united need was no
longer distinguishable. Her hips bucked off the mattress,
her body making its own demands while her mind and
heart simply loved.

With swift movements he removed his clothing and
shoes and leaned over her, his arms coming to rest either side of her face, holding her, cherishing her there.
He pressed the length of his body over hers, the weight
comforting, enticing, and elicited a restlessness from
her body that was almost fevered.

His erection pressed against her abdomen and she
sneaked a hand between them, taking hold of the length
of him, exploring him with her fingers. His skin was
smooth and hot, his arousal powerful, as she stroked
teasing shudders of pleasure from him.

His gaze found hers in the darkness of the room and
no words were necessary. He removed her thong—not
quickly, or urgently, but slowly, pulling the lace slowly
down each thigh, his hands sweeping it further, over
her ankles, taking his time. Not to allow her fears to be
allayed, but her desires to be inflamed.

He came back over her, gold flecks shining in the hot
molten lava churning in his eyes. It seemed for a moment as if he wanted to say something, as if the words
had somehow caught in his throat. But she didn't need
words.

She reached for him then, her hands coming to his
back, urging him to her, urging him into her, and as he
entered her she felt him fill all the empty spaces she

hadn't realised she had until she'd met him. Until she'd seen the man beneath the outer layer he wore about him like armour. Until she'd seen the man he could be.

He pressed deeper, further into her, filling her from the inside out as if they were no longer two people but one. And then there was no room for thought, only sensation. The slick slide of him within her was teasing dizzying need and arousal from her. Pushing her closer and closer to the edge of that same precipice she had sensed him upon.

Lost. He was lost. Antonio was drowning in a sea of emotion and sensation. Emma had cast a spell over him, soothing long-held hurts and filling the spaces with *her.* She was all he could see, all he could feel.

He plunged into her, wringing a cry from her lips, answering the one made by his soul, no longer wanting to think, no longer wanting to hurt. He took her mouth with his, exalting in the sweetness of her, his tongue mirroring his body's actions. He consumed the breath she exhaled, not wanting even that to escape his reach.

Sensation and need became overwhelming as he drove them again and again towards the edge of their release and pulled back. Desperate to stay in this state of bliss, desperate to hold back from the moment it would all come crashing down.

He teased and taunted, wringing pleasure from them both in equal measure. Sweat slicked his brow and hers. The room was filled with the gasps and sighs of exquisite arousal as time suspended its march as if just for them, giving them the simple gift of each other.

But soon need became a palpable thing and he could no longer hold back. He drove them both to the brink, holding them there on the edge. He could taste it on his tongue, in his throat, and hear it in the desperate cries falling from Emma's perfect lips.

With one final thrust he plunged them into the abyss, the joint feeling of their completion sending them into a spin he was sure would never stop.

Antonio woke from the sleep he hadn't realised had fallen over him. He knew before he had even opened his eyes that Emma wasn't with him. It was as if his body had become so attuned to her presence that he no longer needed sight.

And he didn't want to move. Didn't want this moment to happen. Because despite what had just passed between them he knew there was only one outcome— could only ever have been one outcome.

Reluctantly he left the bed, making his way to a bathroom wet with condensation from a shower he hadn't heard Emma take. He couldn't look at himself in the mirror as he stepped beneath the hot spray of water, shutting off the voice that called him a coward in his mind. Whether because of what he would do or couldn't do he didn't know.

Drying himself with a towel, he grabbed his discarded trousers and thrust his legs into them. The fact that only twenty-four hours earlier he had done the same, taken the same action, wasn't lost on him.

The night before he had been about to make a decision that would turn the tide in his battle against his father, no matter the cost. And now he knew instinctively that he would be asked to make the same decision again.

He walked through to the living area of the hotel suite, sidestepping Emma's bags, still packed from hours before. If his heart ached to see them there, he forced it aside.

Emma was sitting on the sofa, illuminated only by the light of dawn breaking over Buenos Aires through the windows. He tried to force a smile to his lips, but couldn't. There wasn't one answering his gaze as she caught sight of his presence.

Antonio was surprised to find that he no longer felt the sting and heat of anger. There was only resignation and sadness for something that was yet to pass. The kind of prescient ache that met inevitability.

'Are you going to use this?' she asked, holding the dossier on Mandy Bartlett.

Emma's heart was torn in two as he stood there, bisected by the shadows of the sunrise. Half in shade, half in light. She wondered which side he would choose. She had asked him the one question she wasn't sure she was ready for him to answer, but knew that she needed hear it.

'If I have to,' he said, and his words made her want to weep.

'Really? You'd destroy this man's family, just like your father did, to get what you want?'

'He deserves it, Emma.'

'Michael might—but does Benjamin Bartlett? Does Mandy?'

She hoped that she could make him see. Before he did something that would change him for ever.

'I will do *whatever* it takes. You already know that.'

She was surprised to hear softness in his voice—not anger, not fury, but gentleness, as if he were preparing her for news she didn't want to hear.

But she wasn't done fighting yet.

'No, I know you, Antonio. I have seen the person beyond the bitter hatred of your father, beyond the fear of the damage done to your sister. I've seen the love you have for her and your mother, the love you have for Dimitri and Danyl. I have seen the man you think you are not, and he is amazing. But if you do this,' she said, hoping against all hope, 'if you use this dossier you will destroy the goodness in you.'

She hated it that she was almost pleading now.

'You don't need to stoop to this level, Antonio. You're better than that. You could win the deal without it. I know it… I know it because I love you.'

Antonio's hand flew up between them, as if warding off her words.

'Don't say that, Emma.'

'Why not? It's the truth. I love you. I can see the man that you are beneath this path of revenge you're on.' She just hated it that he couldn't see it for himself.

'Emma, please—'

'No. You've shown me that all this time I've been hiding. You told me as much last night, when we were together. But it wasn't just my body that I was hiding. And you know that. You knew it then and you know it now. I was hiding from reaching for what I really wanted.'

No longer could Emma hold back the words and thoughts that had been forming, slowly shaping in her mind and heart.

'All this time, all these years, despite my Living List, despite the things I wanted to achieve—events and experiences that are almost meaningless in themselves— what I was really hiding from was love. And now that I *am* reaching for it, asking for it—asking to be loved by you and asking you to be worthy of that—you refuse?' she demanded.

She knew that he felt something for her—possibly even met her love with his own. Whether he would choose that instead of his need for revenge she really wasn't sure. But she knew that their love wouldn't survive if he chose wrong.

'I told you when we first made this deal, Emma, that emotions weren't going to be involved. They *can't* be involved.'

'But emotions are the one thing that's been driving you this whole time!' she cried.

'I can't afford to let my father get away with it. He is a villain, Emma.'

'But are you willing to *become* him to get what you want? Are you willing to become a villain yourself?'

'Emma, if *I* found this, then I guarantee you that my father will have.'

For the first time Emma heard something like desperation enter his voice.

'Then help Bartlett find a way through it,' she said, hoping that Antonio would find a way through his need for revenge. 'Show him the kindness that your father never showed to your mother or you or your sister.'

'I just can't take that risk. I *need* to do this.'

The despair in his voice nearly broke her. Nearly sent her running to this man who had stolen her heart like a thief. But she couldn't—no, she *wouldn't*.

'Then you do it without me.'

She made her way towards the cases by the door, but his words stopped her mid stride.

'It wouldn't have really mattered, though, would it?' he said, his words icy cold and ruthlessly quiet.

'What are you talking about?' she asked, turning towards him, confused at the change in his tone.

'Whether you had discovered this or not. You wouldn't have trusted me—trusted *this*—so you're leaving before you find out.'

'I—'

He didn't let her finish. 'Just like you did to that scared seventeen-year-old boy who might have battled through his fears for you. It's just another excuse to stop yourself from taking a chance.'

Emma felt the blood drain from her face, sucked into the vortex of ice running through her core. *Fear*. She felt fear.

'What is it, Emma? You think we're all going to leave? That we're not strong enough to stick it out with you?'

Antonio's words cut her, chipped away at the frigid centre of her. She hated him then. Hated it that his words were unearthing her deepest fears. The fears she barely allowed herself to admit to owning. The fears that held a mirror up to herself while she threw her accusations at him.

Of course she was scared! She was terrified. Terrified of him using the information in the dossier and even more scared of what it would mean if he *didn't*.

Because then she'd have to stay—really invest—wouldn't she? Not just some giddy, excited fantasy feeling such as she'd been enjoying these last few hours. But the harder stuff—the things that would make her or break her. In that moment she was on the precipice. The edge of a giant cliff-face. One that meant she would have to finally place her trust in someone not to hurt her. Not to leave.

Had she done that? Had she really let her seventeen-year-old boyfriend go without giving him a chance? Was she doing the same again with Antonio?

Her head ached and her mind swam, and in that moment she clung to the only thing she had in front of her.

'You want me to give *what* a chance? Your deal? The

role of fake fiancée? Or could we actually be more than that, Antonio?' she demanded.

It was as if they had become prize fighters, each taking the most painful chunk out of the other.

'There's just six days until the final meeting.'

It seemed neither was willing to admit just how far they'd come, just how much they meant to each other.

She shook her head, her heart breaking into a thousand pieces, the hurt magnified by each fracture, as if punctured by the shards of itself.

'If you can come up with this,' she said, gesturing to the documents that had torn them apart, 'then you can come up with an excuse as to where I am for Bartlett. But, Antonio,' she said—her last warning, her last hope, 'I'm telling you. There's no coming back from this. If you do this you'll be worse than your father. Because you *know* what you're doing, what you're risking, and just how many people you're hurting.'

Antonio didn't move while she retrieved her bags from the doorway to her bedroom. He didn't react to the kiss she placed on his cold cheek and he didn't say a word as she closed the door to the suite behind her.

Emma knew that it was the last time she would see Antonio. Oh, she was sure she would see pictures of him—might even happen upon him in person. But that person wouldn't be the man she had fallen in love with. If he did this—if he used that folder—she would never see that man again.

CHAPTER TEN

ANTONIO HEARD THE pounding on his New York pent-house apartment door and honestly couldn't tell if it was real or the manifestation of his hangover. Each strike followed the words that had been turning over and over in his mind since he last saw Emma.

You'll be worse than your father.

They had become a mantra, a taunt, a final threat hovering over him. One that he couldn't escape. Because he couldn't help feeling that Emma might be right. That in seeking his revenge he would actually be *worse* than his father.

The thought scoured him from the inside out, carved away at the deep ache in his chest.

Reluctant to open his eyes, he turned over and promptly fell onto the floor. The sofa. He'd been on the sofa.

He heard the door swing open and a pair of expensive black leather shoes came to stand very, *very* close to his head. He heard a string of Greek swearing, fit to turn the air blue, and the shoes disappeared. Antonio groaned, knowing that he'd sunk pretty low this time.

He'd been back in New York for two days since returning from Argentina, and in that time he'd answered none of the phone calls from his office, despite the rising panic in his CFO's tone. Instead he'd done nothing but drink and stare at the dossier on a woman he'd never met, might never meet, but who had come to represent the final blow to his relationship with Emma.

Antonio mustered the energy to roll onto his back, every muscle and brain cell protesting. Apart from his heart. His heart relished it, clearly deeming him worthy of such extreme levels of—

Ice-cold water crashed down on his head, the shock making him inhale quickly and deeply, taking half of the liquid into his lungs. He lurched up and bent over, choking and ready to kill Dimitri, holding a now empty jug.

'I've seen you in some pretty bad states, but this is just pitiful.'

'Get out.'

'No.' Dimitri held out a hand and hauled Antonio off the floor.

'Coffee,' was all about Antonio could manage to get out of his mouth.

'Shower,' Dimitri commanded.

It took a moment, but Antonio finally got himself off the floor and made his way through to the kitchen of his apartment, to find Dimitri manhandling a miniature saucepan on the stove.

'Did I fall through the rabbit hole?'

'It's called a *briki*. For an Italian, your coffee equipment is woefully lacking. It's a disgrace.'

'And you just *happened* to have this in your pocket?' Antonio asked, even the image of his friend with a *briki* in his pocket failing to raise a smile to his lips.

Dimitri looked affronted. 'Last year—Christmas. I didn't know what to get you. Emma suggested something that would make you more human in the mornings. It was in the back of your cupboard.'

'And the coffee? It doesn't look like it takes ground beans.'

'That I *did* bring with me.'

Antonio leant back on the kitchen counter that he rarely used and waited as Dimitri poured thick dark liquid into two small coffee cups.

'What are you doing here?' Antonio demanded, thankful that Dimitri ignored the hostility in his tone.

'You didn't answer your phone.'

'What's happened? Is everything okay?'

Panic rose in his chest, filling up the spaces and making it impossible to breathe. Had things got so bad that he had turned his back on his friends? Had something happened to Emma? For just a moment he felt the sliver of guilt as sharp as a chef's knife.

'Well, Danyl's trade negotiations are hanging by a thread, but he'll fix that. My father's company is on the brink, but *I'll* fix that. What are *you* going to do?'

Antonio cursed.

'You really messed this one up,' Dimitri said, casting an angry glance in his direction. 'And Emma is too good a person to mess with. So get in the shower. You smell like self-pity and alcohol and I don't like it. Be quick.'

Antonio forced himself under the hot water jets of his powerful shower. But it did nothing to remove the taint of dark grime he felt on his skin—had felt ever since seeing the photos of Mandy Bartlett his PI had dug up…ever since Emma had walked away from him.

Antonio decided to leave his hair wet. Although he was feeling much better, rubbing his head didn't seem that appealing. He entered his kitchen to find Dimitri poring over the images in the folder on Mandy Bartlett, and felt oddly furious that yet another person had seen them.

'Damaging stuff.'

'Yes,' Antonio practically growled, feeling oddly proprietorial over the contents of the folder…over Mandy's downward descent.

'Girl needs some sense knocked into her.'

'She needs help, Dimitri.'

'Yeah. Not sure her father will give it to her if he gets hold of these, though,' Dimitri mused. 'So Emma's gone, then?'

'Yes.'

'A shame. I like her.'

Antonio felt himself bristle.

'Don't be stupid—not in *that* way. So you can put the caveman back in the box.'

Antonio took a sip of the rich, peaty coffee, almost scalding his tongue in the process. He wasn't sure whether he was ready to hear what Dimitri had to say, but he knew Dimitri would say it anyway.

'Look, I know how much this deal means to you. I know your need for revenge, Antonio—trust me,' said Dimitri. 'I really do. And I will support whatever decision you make. Because you're my brother. You're my family. I don't believe those people who say you can't pick your family because I can and I have. You and Danyl—you're it. Whatever you choose to do with Bartlett is your own matter. I'm not here about the deal. I'm here about *her*.'

And finally all the resistance, all the avoidance that he'd practised since Emma had left him in the hotel suite in Argentina, dropped away.

'She held a mirror up to me, Dimitri. And I didn't like what I saw,' he admitted finally. The ache in his chest was opening up into a river of pain. 'The horror in her face…the betrayal… I don't think I can come back from that.'

'We all have to face the darkest parts of ourselves at some point, Antonio.'

There was no judgement in Dimitri's eyes, but in a way it only served to enrich the last memories he had of Emma and all the emotion he had seen in *her* eyes.

'Do you love her?'

'Yes. I do,' he replied—without thought, without pause.

He'd known it when he'd gone to the hotel suite that last night in Buenos Aires—known it as he'd allowed her to walk away from him. Had known it because it had hurt more than any other single thing in his life.

She had offered him everything. Love, acceptance, a way forward—a way other than the path of his revenge—and he had refused it all. He had refused *her*.

'Then you do what it takes, Antonio.'

'Even if that means letting go of the feud I have with my father?'

Emma pulled the cotton robe around her shoulders as she sank into her mother's sofa in the small house in Hampstead Heath. She had flown back into London four days ago and had slept for practically all of them, as if her body's learned response to trauma—emotional or physical—was rest.

So much had changed since she'd last left this house. Not only for her, but for her mother. Her old bedroom was now the spill-over storage area for Mark's hobby—his cars. Spare bits of machinery, cases of tools, several worn, torn and oil-stained clothes hung over the corners of barely held together boxes.

She was surprised to find that it didn't upset her. She was glad that her mother had found Mark—a kind man who loved her deeply. How could she begrudge her mother the very thing she wanted for herself? But every time she thought of Antonio her heart ached a little more. She knew that she was feeling grief—grief for him, for herself. But even through that pain, the exhaustion and the upset, she knew that she should get up every day and fight for the future she had once closed herself off from.

The sitting room was still just how she'd remembered it. Books lining two sides of the room, paintings framing the windows on the front wall, and covering the back wall completely, as if they were puzzle pieces, separated by only the thinnest of gaps of wall. It felt familiar—but not as soothing as it had once been.

Her mother entered the room, her jeans and loose shirt covered in mismatched blotches of cast-off paint, thin lines from where she had cleaned the pallet knife she used against her thighs.

Louise Guilham was beautiful. Emma had inherited her mother's thick dark hair and slender form. But it wasn't her physical appearance that made her beautiful. It was her happiness in following her dream of painting, in her love for Mark. It glowed from her skin and Emma felt sallow and shadowed in comparison.

She mustered a smile as her mother looked momentarily confused to find Emma curled up on the sofa at five in the afternoon, a robe wrapped around clothes she had slept in, not having had the energy to change. That was her mother's way when she was locked into a painting. The world could descend into Armageddon and she'd still be considering which colour to put where.

'Would you like a cup of tea?' Louise asked.

'I don't suppose you have any whisky?' Emma replied, memories of a conversation with Antonio so very close to the surface of her thoughts.

Her mother raised an eyebrow, but disappeared into the kitchen, returning with two glasses full of ice and amber.

'Do you want to talk about it?' she asked Emma, pressing the glass into her hands and taking a seat beside her on the old, battered but comfortable sofa.

Emma turned, resting her back against the sofa's arm, stretching out her legs. Her mother took Emma's feet in her hands and put them on her lap, passing soothing strokes over her bare skin as she had once done so many times when Emma had been ill.

Over the last four days, between hours of sleep, Emma had unfolded the story of her and Antonio, opening her heart and her mind to the mother she wouldn't hide a thing from—ever. But now Emma felt the stirrings of the question she had always wanted to ask and never had the courage to.

Until now.

'Not about Antonio, no. But I want to talk to you about Dad.'

'Oh? Okay.'

Mark hovered in the doorway. He must have heard Emma's question, and now he sent them both a gentle smile. He announced that he was *'just going to pop to the pub'*, and left them alone, free to talk openly.

Yet another thing for which she was grateful to Mark.

'Mum, was it my fault that you and Dad split up? Was it because I got ill?'

'Oh, Em,' her mother said. 'How long have you thought that?'

'Since it happened,' Emma admitted guiltily.

'Oh, my love. No. No, it wasn't your fault at all—and neither was it because of the cancer,' she said, both sincerity and sadness in her voice.

Her mother's attention drifted to the window and she sighed.

'Your father and I met and married when we were very young. We loved each other greatly. And when you came along we loved you even more. But unlike some couples who are able to grow together, grow *up* together, we just...*didn't*,' she said, with a small shrug of her shoulders.

'So you stayed together because I got sick? That's even worse,' Emma said, guilt piercing her already fractured heart.

'No, sweetheart, we stayed together because we loved *you*,' her mother said, her voice and tone adamant and powerful. 'And that love was a strong, beautiful amazing thing that saw us all through the darkest of times. Neither me nor your father would change a day of it.'

Emma felt a huge weight lift from her chest as the fear that had been holding her back for so long left and was replaced with the truth in her mother's words.

Looking back, it was as if the memories that she had always shied away from had been freshly painted over, dusted in fine golden light, showing her different images. Where once she had felt guilt and sadness, she now felt strength and light. Seeing the way that they had stayed together as a gift.

And in that moment she realised that Antonio had been right. She *had* been running away from him. Consumed by her own fears, she had run away from her feelings. She had not stayed with Antonio when he had most needed her. Worse, she had done the very thing she had always been scared that someone would do to her.

'Oh, Mum...' Emma couldn't help the cry falling

from her lips. 'I left him…' she said, tears trembling at the edges of her eyes.

Her mother laid a reassuring hand on her legs. 'From what you told me, Emma, he had a decision to make and he had to make it by himself.'

'Mum, I love you. So, so very much. But I have to go.'

Antonio resisted the urge to place a finger between his collar and his neck in an attempt to loosen the feeling of a noose tightening around him. He could not— *would* not—show any sign of weakness in front of his father *or* Bartlett.

They were in the boardroom at Bartlett's sleek offices, just a few blocks over from Antonio's own office. That he was being forced to breathe the same air as his father angered him. But he had to let that anger go. Bartlett had promised a decision today, after final pitches from himself and Michael Steele, in a move that was both highly unusual and had taken on the air of a courtroom with closing arguments.

His father had blustered through his determined statements—more of the same kind of financial arguments that had been printed in the world's international press over the last week. About how Michael's age and experience gave more weight to his investment and the promise that he could best his son financially.

Which he couldn't.

But apparently the more he said it, the more Michael thought Bartlett would believe it. Michael had also made asinine suggestions as to Antonio's scandalous reputation and the damage it would do to Bartlett's company—in spite of his recent, perhaps even *conve-*

nient engagement—and once again Antonio's anger that his father should involve Emma in this had been swift.

But just as swift was the recrimination that he had brought Emma into it himself.

Antonio took a moment, after his father had finished, and Bartlett turned his attention to him. He checked his feelings, checked his decision and felt at peace. Possibly for the first time in years.

'So much has been said about the strength, might and determination that got my father here,' Antonio began. 'About how he's the right man to invest in your company and see it into the future. But I disagree. And not just because I don't believe him for a second.'

He pushed the threads of anger aside, holding on to the purpose of his intention for the meeting. Holding on to the memory, the realisation of what Emma had shown him.

'It's not very often that business deals come down to right and wrong. You're a man of strong morals, Mr Bartlett,' he said, holding the older man's gaze, needing him to see the truth of the words he was about to say. 'And if I'm honest—*truly* honest—I can't say the same of myself.'

He saw the shock on Bartlett's face, heard the small gasp that spoke of his confusion at a man appearing to sabotage his own pitch.

'I came after this deal not because I want to invest in your company, Mr Bartlett, but because I want my father not to.'

He didn't have to look at his father to know that he was practically vibrating with glee—he could feel it in the air, the drop in temperature from Bartlett's end of the room matching the raised heat from his father's.

'And in order to do that I betrayed and treated badly

a woman of such high integrity that she would put us all to shame. She certainly put *me* to shame,' he admitted, feeling the words ring true in his heart. 'She showed me that I was reaching only for revenge when what I should have been reaching for was to be *better* than him— better than my father. A better man for myself and the woman I love. I did and still do want to invest in your company, Mr Bartlett. But not at the price of my morals or my heart. And I should warn you that if you choose my father, you'll be selling your soul to the devil. Make your decision, Benjamin. And once you have—whatever it is—there is a matter I'd like to discuss with you. One that I'd like to help with, if you'll let me.'

With that, Antonio got up from his chair and turned—expecting to leave, expecting to walk out into the sunshine of a New York summer, expecting to track down Emma wherever she might be and beg her forgiveness.

But it seemed she had other ideas.

Emma was standing in the doorway of the board-room, and his first thought was how truly amazing she looked.

Her eyes shone, and her hair was loose around her shoulders—it was the first time he'd seen it so during the day, outside of the nights of passion they had shared. She was dressed in a brightly coloured dress that hugged her chest and waist, flared about her legs, and a simply outrageous and uncharacteristically Emma pair of high heels encased her feet.

But it was exactly how he'd always imagined her. Bright, feminine, sensual and powerful.

'How much did you hear?' he asked, walking towards her, hoping that she wasn't a figment of his fevered imagination.

'Everything,' she said, allowing him to guide her away from the office.

He couldn't take his eyes from her—couldn't bring himself to say another word until they were free from the office, the deal, his father. He wanted to leave it all behind him.

Well, not *all*. He had meant what he'd said to Bartlett. Once the deal was made—whether Bartlett chose him or not—Antonio wanted to speak to the man about his daughter. He either knew and wasn't sure how to proceed, or he didn't know and would need help and support to get through to her. But Antonio wouldn't allow the situation with Mandy Bartlett to go unchecked.

They emerged from the office onto the sidewalk and, still without a word, he took her hand and led her as quickly as her heels would allow across the road, towards the lower entrance of Central Park. He wanted life, greenery and peace to be the background of their next conversation. Not the high-rise hustle and bustle of Manhattan.

Walking away from the summer crowds of tourists gathering around the ice-cream sellers and busking musicians, Antonio drew them towards the quieter pathways, dappled with leafy shade and cool breeze. But when he got where he'd wanted to be he suddenly found himself unsure. What if she didn't want him? What if his decision hadn't made any difference to her feelings?

In the end it seemed that Emma found her courage before he did. She stopped, gently pulling on his arm, turning her towards him.

'Antonio, I'm so sorry that I left you,' she said. 'I never—'

'Don't be sorry,' he interrupted, hating it that she felt an ounce of sadness or regret about the actions that had forced him to confront his feelings in a way that nothing else had. 'I needed to see the true depths of the darkness I was about to fall into before I could reach for you, before I could reach for the light.'

He paused, hoping that she understood his words, took them into her as deeply as he meant them.

'I want to be worthy of you, Emma. I want to be better than him. I am now and will continue to be. Whether you'll do me the honour of becoming my wife or not. I know you will—'

'Wait,' she said, throwing up a hand between them. 'What?' she asked.

He cursed, realising that he'd blundered over the most important thing he'd ever asked in his life. The first time they had done this it had been for the deal. This time he wanted it to be a moment that she cherished, that she remembered, might even tell their children about one day.

'Emma, I love you. So very much,' he said, digging into his pocket for the small box he'd arranged to have sent over from the shop in Buenos Aires. 'I know you heard what I said in the room with Bartlett and my father—but I want you to hear it now. Here, without them present, not for show or for a deal, but for *you*. For years I've shied away from love, from meaningful relationships, because I thought that love was a destructive, harmful thing. Something my father used against my mother—something that left my sister destroyed when it was withdrawn from her. And something that left me with my own scars. But that wasn't true. You showed me, that last night in Argentina and in so many ways preceding it, that love is a healing, powerful, amazing thing. I know now that what my father did wasn't borne of love. And no matter what happens—whether you say yes or not—I want you to know that I love you, and I will love you every single day for the rest of my life if you will let me.'

He got down on one knee, drawing the curious gazes of some of the few people passing by. And it was then that Emma truly knew the power of their love as it washed over them both from his words, his eyes, his heart.

'Emma Guilham,' he said, taking her hand in his, 'would you do me the incredible honour of being my wife?' he asked, sending her heart soaring higher than she had ever felt.

She couldn't help the laugh that escaped her lips, but she too had words she wanted to share. Things she wanted him to understand so that they could move ahead with all the love and security she knew they would both feel.

She gently tugged at him, attempting to pull him up from where he knelt. And she laughed again when he shook his head and refused, drawing even more attention from the people passing.

'If you won't stand then I shall have to come down to you,' she taunted.

'So be it. I will not move until I've had your answer,' he said, a stubborn determination filling his words in a blissful promise that she wouldn't have thought him capable of when she'd first met him.

So she did as she had said and took to her knees, facing him, holding her gaze with his and, just like Antonio, not caring of the attention they were drawing.

'For so long I thought myself strong, capable—no,' she said as he tried to interrupt her, knowing that he would contradict her words, but knowing too that she needed to say them. 'I was, am and will continue to be a survivor. But for all the promise and hope put into that list I made as a seventeen-year-old, I never had the courage to ask for the things that I truly wanted. Self-acceptance, self-love and ultimately true love itself. Antonio, you showed me that my scars are beautiful, you taught me to reach for the things I was too scared and too unwilling to admit to myself that I wanted, and you proved to me that doing so, whether successful or not, was the real gift. You showed me that it was okay— more than that, *vital* for me to put my whole self out into the world. And I love you for it, and I will love you for it until my last breath. So, yes, Antonio Arcuri, I *will* marry you.'

The moment the words had left her mouth Antonio pulled Emma to him in a kiss that she would never forget. It was full of the taste of love, passion and everything in between. It was full of light, laughter and finally, the knowledge that they would live happily ever after.

EPILOGUE

One year later...

ARCURI WELCOMES THE
BIRTH OF HIS SON!
BY ROANNA KING

**International tycoon announces the
birth of a beautiful baby boy!**

*Hearts across the world might have burned with
envy at the pictures of Antonio Arcuri's wedding
only four months ago. The shocking speed not only
of his engagement to Emma Guilham—his one-time
PA—but his subsequent marriage raised more than
a few eyebrows amongst our hallowed readership.*

*One could argue that the reason for this was
the soon-to-follow birth of their son, little Luca
Arcuri. But that would be an argument from a
harder heart than mine.*

*Because it's clear to see the love shining in the
eyes of this proud papa, and I can only wish them
luck in their future endeavours.*

*So let me be the first to congratulate you, Mr
Arcuri, on the wonderful birth of your son.*

EMMA ENTERED THE large open-plan living room of their house in Sorrento, with her gorgeous son Luca cradled in her arms, to find Antonio talking to himself.

'*"Harder heart than mine..."*' he muttered angrily. '*"Let me be the first..."* Really, how dare she?'

Antonio threw yet another one of Roanna King's articles into the bin.

Emma laughed—something she did so very much these days—and crossed the room to pull him into a kiss that wasn't nearly as deep as she'd like, but perfectly respectable given there were three of them squashed into each other's arms.

'How dare who?'

'Mmm?' he asked, as he took in the sight of his wife and child. 'I've forgotten—not important.'

And he meant it. All he had ever wanted was here in this room.

So much had changed in the year since he had discovered Bartlett wanted investment in his company—since he'd demanded that Emma find him a fiancée. At the time he'd thought that what he'd wanted was revenge, to destroy his father. But things hadn't quite turned out that way.

Soon after his *second* proposal to Emma, Benjamin Bartlett had got in touch. Apparently Michael Steele had tried to use the information about his daughter against him, but instead of buckling to the demands he'd made Bartlett had stuck to his instincts, turned to Antonio instead, and together they had worked to help Mandy Bartlett weather the storm that Michael Steele had launched upon the poor girl.

Sometimes Antonio very much wished that he'd found a way to avoid that for Bartlett and his family, but Antonio was beginning to realise that accepting the consequences of one's actions was an important part of the healing process.

Bartlett's shares had wobbled for a few days under the negative press, but with Antonio's investment they'd soon recovered. With Antonio, Emma and her father's support, Mandy Bartlett had gone into rehab and ended up finishing her degree and passing with high honours, and the Bartletts were now a firm fixture in their social calendar.

And as for Michael Steele—it hadn't taken long for the press to turn against the man. Once they'd discovered that it had been *he* who had leaked the dossier about Mandy's troubles, and there had been the suggestion—though unproved and unsupported—that it had been in retaliation for a rejected business venture, it had sickened the international press.

Hounded and stalked by their fury that he could abuse such an innocent young girl, Michael had found his existing business associates driving as far from him as possible. The man had become a financial and social pariah—though Antonio had been surprised to discover that it hadn't felt as good as he'd thought. It had been a period that had been difficult for Antonio, when he'd realised just how far he had nearly sunk himself. But Emma had helped him through with patient love, sweet comfort and reassurance.

Shortly after Antonio had made good on his first promise to Emma, and the Bartletts had been present, alongside Dimitri and Danyl, to toast Emma's new role as head of the Arcuri Foundation—celebrations that had gone on long into the night, full of joy, laughter and hope for the future.

Despite their busy schedule, they had already ticked off several of the things on Emma's Living List. Even now, standing in their home in Sorrento, he remembered the exquisite joy in Emma's eyes as they'd shared a sunrise over the Terhren desert, and the happiness shining just as bright when they'd seen the sun set over the Mediterranean, surrounded by their closest friends, Danyl and Dimitri, and their respective families.

'Where are you?' Emma asked, and smiled as she passed his son to him.

'Right here, where I should be,' replied Antonio, drawing his thoughts away from the past and holding their precious son to his chest.

He watched Emma, stepping over the changing mat and the stacks of muslins, nappies and other little things he'd never thought to find such joy in, as she went to the mirror that covered almost the entire length of one wall. He watched her as she checked her hair and her brightly coloured dress. He never tired of seeing her in autumn colours, and he was sure that he hadn't seen her wear black since Buenos Aires.

He gently put his sleeping son in the small bassinette beside the sofa, already missing the soft, gentle comfort of having him in his arms, and walked to his wife, unable to resist the urge to hold her, touch her. He wondered if he ever would.

He pressed a starburst of kisses along the beautiful length of her neck, knowing Emma would understand the gesture and the silent, sensual request behind it.

Emma playfully slapped his arms away from her. 'You know we don't have time, Antonio. Danyl and Dimitri will be here with their families in little over two hours, and Danyl's protection services always make such a drama about the whole thing—they'll be at the door in twenty minutes.'

'Having a sheikh as a friend has both its perks and its curses,' Antonio growled.

That each of the Winners' Circle had found happiness and love within the space of such a short time was still a marvel to all three men. But those were stories for another time. For now, Antonio's only thought was of his wife, and just what he could do with twenty little minutes.

A wicked smile crept across his face, and Emma soon discovered that twenty minutes could be just as pleasurable as a lifetime.

* * * * *

MILLS & BOON

Coming next month

CONSEQUENCE OF
THE GREEK'S REVENGE
Trish Morey

'Going somewhere, Athena?'

Breath hitched in her lungs as every nerve receptor in her body screeched in alarm. Alexios!

How did he know she was here?

She wouldn't turn around. She wouldn't look back, forcing herself to keep moving forwards, her hand reaching for the door handle and escape, when his hand locked on her arm, a five fingered manacle, and once again she tasted bile in her throat, reminding her of the day she'd thrown up outside his offices. The bitter taste of it incensed her, spinning her around.

'Let me go!' She tried to stay calm, to keep the rising panic from her voice. Because if he knew she was here, he must surely know why, and she was suddenly, terribly, afraid. His jaw was set, his eyes were unrepentant, and they scanned her now, as if looking for evidence, taking inventory of any changes. There weren't any, not that anyone else might notice, though she'd felt her jeans grow more snug just lately, the beginnings of a baby bump.

'We need to talk.'

'No!' She twisted her arm, breaking free. 'I've got nothing to say to you,' she said, rubbing the place where his hand had been, still scorchingly hot like he had used a searing brand against her skin, rather than just his fingers.

'No?' His eyes flicked up to the brass plate on near the door, to the name of the doctor in obstetrics. 'You didn't think I might be interested to hear that you're pregnant with my child?'

Continue reading
CONSEQUENCE OF
THE GREEK'S REVENGE
Trish Morey

Available next month
www.millsandboon.co.uk

COMING SOON!

We really hope you enjoyed reading this book. If you're looking for more romance, be sure to head to the shops when new books are available on

Thursday
4th October

To see which titles are coming soon, please visit
millsandboon.co.uk

LET'S TALK
Romance

For exclusive extracts, competitions
and special offers, find us online:

 facebook.com/millsandboon

@millsandboonuk

@millsandboon

Or get in touch on 0844 844 1351*

For all the latest titles coming soon, visit
millsandboon.co.uk/nextmonth